H

SIMON &
SCHUSTER

NEW YORK

LONDON

TORONTO

SYDNEY

SINGAPORE

YOLANDA JOE

Writing as
**ARDELLA
GARLAND**

HIT TIME

A MYSTERY

SIMON & SCHUSTER
Rockefeller Center
1230 Avenue of the Americas
New York, NY 10020

SIMON & SCHUSTER and colophon are registered trademarks
of Simon & Schuster, Inc.

Designed by Barbara M. Bachman
Manufactured in the United States of America

1   3   5   7   9   10   8   6   4   2

Library of Congress Cataloging-in-Publication Data
Garland, Ardella, date.
        Hit time : a mystery / Yolanda Joe writing as Ardella Garland.
                p.   cm.
        1. African American television journalists—Fiction.   2. Women
television journalists—Fiction.   3. African American women—
Fiction.   4. Chicago (Ill.)—Fiction.   5. Music trade—Fiction.
I. Title.
PS3560.O242 H58 2002
813'.54—dc21   2001054956
                        ISBN 0-684-87376-1

For information regarding special discounts for bulk purchases,
please contact Simon & Schuster Special Sales at 1-800-456-6798
or business@simonandschuster.com

Acknowledgments

Words can hardly express the joy I feel for all the support

I have received on this project. So I will simply say thanks

and love ya much to Constance, Stephen, Nicole, Tracy,

and as always, *mighty-mighty* Victoria.

Story Slug = Cold Charity
5 P.M. *Show, December 3rd*

ANCHOR INTRO
(DAN READS)

CLOSE-UP

The American Heart Association is telling the Elite Swim Club to go jump in the lake.

Literally.

Once again it's time for the club's annual charity event, the Winter Relay. Club members have collected $10,000 in pledges this year.

WJIV's Georgia Barnett is live at the lakefront with details.

Georgia?

(*********STOP*********)

TAKE LIVE SHOT
CHYRON LOCATION: LIVE/MANNING PIER
LIVE/GEORGIA BARNETT/CHANNEL 8 NEWS

(GEORGIA LIVE)

Dan, we are having unseasonably warm weather for December. Today's high was around 50 degrees. But that'll do little to knock the chill off the ice-cold waters of Lake Michigan.

The race is now in its tenth year. A swimmer will start at the pier, go out to that buoy and back, then the next swimmer will take off.

As you can see behind me, I'm surrounded by family and friends of the Elite Swim Club. They're here to cheer on their loved ones for charity.

(NATURAL SOUND/CROWD CHEERS)

The swimmers are lined up. The official is ready to start.

**(CROWD COUNTS DOWN/
STARTER PISTOL SHOT)**

And they're off! Wow, look at them go!

**(NATURAL SOUND RACE/
WIDE SHOT)**

Now if you, the Channel 8 audience, would like to help the Elite Swim Club reach its goal by making a donation call the number on the bottom of your screen....

**(PANDEMONIUM IN WATER/
WIDE SHOT)**

Something's ... something's wrong ... I can't tell ... the swimmers are coming back. They're panicking!

(VARIOUS SWIMMERS SHOUTING)

Oh my God! Help! There's a body! It's a man! A dead body in the lake! Oh my God!

WHAT A TRIPPED-OUT WAY TO START A WORKWEEK.

Monday afternoon I went out to do a live shot about a charity event, a simple feel-good story—an *easy-pleasy* I call it. That *easy-pleasy* turned ugly-wugly right there during my live shot with three hundred thousand viewers watching.

Eyeballing the ugly.

We stayed hot with the coverage. I was live. When the police arrived—when they pulled the body out of the water. My ace cameraman, Zeke Rouster, was all over the video, getting shots of the scene from various angles. I was hustling. I was giving detailed descriptions about every little thing that was going on. I sounded like a sportscaster except my play-by-play involved divers, detectives, and dead men.

Dead men tell no tales.

Or answer any questions either for that matter.

Like . . . who was this man? Was this an accident? A suicide? Or could it be murder?

It's like a TV game show, except there's no Regis and no grand prize. The viewers follow the story intently as it unfolds, waiting for the right answers, wondering how it'll all turn out. And it's a hard game to play too except for the people who must . . . like the police and the press.

In this case that would be my boyfriend Doug and me. Who knows how many twists and turns this news story will take before winding down to the truth. Who knows?

Chapter One

LIKE A FISH OUT OF WATER, I WATCHED THIS DEAD BODY sag in the hands of those who hauled it out of Lake Michigan. The deceased had on black pants, a red-and-black-checkered jacket with big flap pockets. In those pockets were bricks soaked clean from being in the water.

Had this man figured that he could weigh himself down with a few bricks, hoping that their weight and the weight of his desire for death would be enough to sink him?

If the dude was going for suicide, he rang the bell and won the prize.

If a killer was trying to hide the deed, the mark was badly missed.

This body had found its way near shore. The *who* and the *how* of it was a puzzle for cops and journalists to figure out. I was struck by the man's hands: green, next to frigid blue, next to bruised red. Without question I was eyeballing the combination quilt work of death and water. The damage those two bad boys can do together on the human flesh is more than a notion.

And this stiff wasn't a young cat either; he had gray hair, cut close, and brown age spots speckled his thick neck and sloping chin. His white skin was stained a sickly yellow. The skin, that's the first thing that takes a major hit when you die. The skin. Gives up the ghost like it ain't nothing. Turning flat. Stiff. Hardly showing signs that there was ever any life at all.

My favorite cameraman, Zeke Rouster, was standing behind me getting a pan shot from the victim's head to his toes. Zeke then did a squat and grunted so loud I almost laughed. His jelly stomach went from three months pregnant to six; a sistah wouldah cracked on him if the situation wasn't so doggone grave.

One of the detectives rolled the victim on his side and water sloshed out of his ear. Zeke was a film fiend, panning and zooming, catching close-ups and cutaway shots of the club members still huddled together in awe of the tragedy playing out before them.

"It's not pretty is it, Zeke?"

"Never is, Georgia," he said, flipping on the camera's overhead light. Zeke grunted again as he stood up, then took a swing at a stubborn section of white hair that kept falling into his face. "I'm getting too old for this shit."

"Not a chance, Zeke. Old cameramen never retire, they just fade to black. You're still the best shooter in town."

"Edit text. You mean the planet."

Zeke is about as modest as a nude baby on a bear rug. He loves to be stroked. I don't mind stroking him either, because he deserves it. Zeke is a news cowboy ready to go anywhere and do whatever it takes to get the story right. He has paid a stack of dues too over his many years and always has my back. Like now . . .

"Yo, Georgia," Zeke said, giving me one of his mischievous green-eyed winks, "here comes Detective Love Jones!"

Zeke was a teasing somebody. I didn't want to smile but, doggone it, I did. Before I even looked up, I knew Zeke was talking about Detective Doug Eckart. Obviously he'd caught this case. We hadn't worked the same incident since a little girl named Butter disappeared in late summer. On that case we initially bumped heads, then put our heads together, and eventually our hearts.

Doug glanced in my direction but played it cool. We didn't want our business in the street. The top cops Doug needed to impress to move up the ranks might not like our relationship, and my rival colleagues might cry foul thinking I'm gleaning inside info between the sheets.

"Clear that camera back," Doug said to the police support crew. "This is a crime scene, not a movie."

Zeke sarcastically sucked his teeth.

"Suck 'em any harder and you'll need braces!" Doug barked.

The cops all laughed.

Zeke rolled his eyes at Doug. Then he hunched his shoulders at me as if to say, *Get your boy in check.*

But I had no issue with Doug. It was mandatory that he take charge. And he wasn't hurting us a smidgen. We'd already done three live updates. We were also assured the lead story spot at six.

"Don't fret," I said lightly patting Zeke's back. "We're beating everybody on this story."

I moved to get an interview with Erin, one of the swimmers who had dived in and made the grisly discovery. Erin was badly shaken up, so much so that after she got out of the water her voice vanished.

Speechless and trembling like a dry leaf, Erin was comforted by her friends. I made sure the paramedic gave her a good looking-over. Now Erin stood off to the side with a grave marker on her shoulders—face stony, eyes hard, lips engraved in a frown.

"Erin, we're about to go live, can you please just give us a minute?" It took several seconds for what I'd said to register. Girlfriend was shaken up for real! It'd be more than a minute before Erin would feel good about sleeping with the lights off again. Her electric bill would be mighty high.

"Yes, sure, I can talk . . . a little." Erin forced the corners of her mouth to turn up ever so slightly. Then she ran a nervous hand over her shiny brown hair, slick with lake water.

Zeke set up behind me, balanced the camera on his knees, framed the shot up, giving her depth, adding more intensity to her words.

"Turn your body left." Zeke made two backhanded swipes with his hand. "Good. That's perfect."

We got set for a live update. The director cued me in my earpiece and I was on. I gave a quick intro recapping the charity event that led to the grisly discovery. Then I did TV news like it should be done. I let Erin tell the story just as she'd experienced it—up close and personal.

·

"I was in the water, you know? It stung, the coldness of it. I was a championship diver in college, so I know how to get control of my body under water. I went a bit deep, then I began to float up. I pulled away from the rest of the swimmers. As I got closer to the buoy, that's when I saw it. . . ."

Like metal to a magnet, Erin's fingertips were drawn to her lips. She gulped twice before continuing her story.

"I looked and there he . . . was . . . this man . . . his hair floating like seaweed or something, helpless-looking, arms out, dead as can be."

"Erin, can you remember your first reaction and what you were thinking at that moment?"

"I screamed and swallowed a little bit of water. It took every fiber of my being to stay calm. I kept thinking, I gotta get out of this water, back to shore, get help. Then everyone was yelling. It was chaotic. I can't tell you how upsetting . . . how—how . . ."

Then Erin began to cry. I gently put my arm around her shoulder and closed off my live shot.

"The police are here on the scene trying to determine if this is an accident, a suicide, or a homicide. Right now it is classified as a death investigation. The identity of the victim remains a mystery. We will update the story as more information becomes available. Georgia Barnett, live at Manning Pier. Back to you in the newsroom."

Out of the corner of my eye I saw Doug examining the body. The boy has skills. A few times Doug has talked to me about some of his old cases. Intent and deliberate, he had explained to me how the investigations went—how something minute captured his attention and just wouldn't let go. Those kinds of things were always the prologue to the case, Doug told me. The beginning. The beginning that started you on the path to the end.

I worked on my long story, or package as we call it, adding more interviews from the swim club members.

I also interviewed Doug. By then other television reporters were there, some scowling and others smiling, giving me my props, not for catching a story that fell right into my lap, as it most certainly had, but for knowing how to run and score with that bad boy once I had it.

Doug was keeper of the info. All of the reporters surrounded him, a gang-bang as we call it in the business. The questions hit him rapidly. Doug deflected and dodged those questions like a championship boxer, only unleashing powerful tips when he was ready. I let my colleagues lead.

"Whatcha got, Detective Eckart?"

"A short time ago this case changed from a death investigation to a murder investigation."

"You ruled out an accident or suicide pretty quickly."

"Well, it's pretty hard to shoot yourself in the back."

"Multiple gunshot wounds?"

"Two shots."

Then I began asking more pointed questions as I stood in the crowd, thinking, remembering what the dead man looked like fresh out of the water. The front of the torso remained clean, besides, of course, the water damage. There were no exit wounds in the front.

"Detective," I asked, "were the shots fired from a great distance or from a small-caliber gun? There were no exit wounds on the body."

Doug's eyes smiled. *Yeah, baby, you've been listening to me and the boys chatter.*

"The weapon in this case appears to be a small-caliber. Yes."

"Was this a robbery?"

"That is a possible motive. The victim did not have a wallet or anything containing identification on his body."

So it was very likely a robbery. But why go to all the trouble of moving the body? This pier is pretty secluded in the winter, so who-ever brought the body down to Manning Pier had a good chance of not being seen. True. But why would a regular old stickup ace do that?

Doug began giving a description of the victim—white male, sixty to sixty-five years old, five nine, muscular build, 170 pounds, gray hair, brown eyes, wearing a red-and-black jacket, black pants and shoes—all before wrapping up the gang-bang.

"Right now the investigation is moving forward, the body is in the capable hands of the coroner. As we get new information that we can pass on to you, we will do so."

That was cop slang for, *Get out my face now 'cause I got work to do.*

We gave Detective Ace some space. Reporting crime stories is easy in the beginning. Clues are few. There's not a lot to sift through yet. Every reporter there—from NBC, ABC, WGN, and FOX on down—ended their live shots the same. And that was with a physical description of the victim and a plea to the public for help; if anyone thought they knew the victim or if they'd seen something strange in the area around Manning Pier, they should call the police.

I waited for Zeke to give me a ride back to WJIV after our last live shot. Usually I tried to grab a cab or drive my own car if I could instead of hanging around until Zeke finished meticulously packing up all the equipment.

But I was in no rush tonight. You see, Doug and I had an after-work date, but by now our after-work plans were out of whack. We both had expected a light workday. We both got our heads bumped by reality.

I was truly an unhappy sister. Had tickets to the Symphony Center to see the dynamic diva Leontyne Price. Now our work was jamming us up like a fender-bender during rush hour. Don't you just hate it when a funky workday interferes with your personal life?

So Doug and I ended up skipping dinner and the performance. Instead we would hook up late and kick back at my twin sister's place, the Blues Box.

Chapter Two

AWWW, IF YOU GONNA WALK ON MY LOVIN', THE LEAST YOU
could do is take off your shoes!! Awww, baby!"

My twin sister, Peaches, torched out the blues standard. The
place was packed. Professional night-lifers ruled the roost. They
wore the finest clothes, had the latest haircuts, wore the coolest
hats, and sported the flyest jewelry. They looked good and they were
rocking. Their bodies bobbed up and down like ice cubes buoyed in
whiskey.

Doug and I were snuggling in a back booth of the Blues Box. The
powder blue vinyl seats showed every bit of their secondhand
nature. But I wasn't uncomfortable. Not a smidgen. My padding was
the curve in Doug's hips, the cushion in that hidden soft spot of his
body that lay just under his arm.

I could see our reflection in the large mirror, centered over the
main bar. His strong shoulders were relaxed, his dark skin and the
chiseled features of his face were in sync with the sultry atmosphere
of the club. My long legs were stretched out. I wanted to kick off my
shoes, but doggone it if ah sister like me even dared! I'm on air, and
people are always recognizing me.

I could hear the conversation now, *"Girl, I was in my little spot over
there on Pershing Road—yeah, the blues joint. Well, the black reporter on*

Channel 8—not him—the tall, thin, light brown sister? Her twin owns the place and they don't look nothing alike! Anyway, the reporter sister, Georgia Barnett, she was sitting up in there looking just as tacky. Do you know she had her shoes off? Showing some ugly toes but all hugged up with a fine man. Girl, I ain't even lying."

That's what I call *P-Funk*—when the public won't let you be a regular person and gets oh so cruel about it. My undercover corns would just have to continue to suffer undercover.

But Peaches was front and center. She takes full command whenever she's onstage. The crowd had taken a pure interest in every move she made. Peaches wailed while rolling her shoulders, pumping lofty hips, swaying her behind, moving with unabashed power over such a vast space that she could have formed her own galaxy. Upon future discovery by scientists it could only be named one thing—*The Constellation of Do That.*

"This is my spot," I purred. "Peaches throws down for real when she gets onstage. That girl can sing her butt off."

"Not to mention we get the best seats in the house!" Doug squeezed me. "That's cool."

I happily agreed, then my thoughts turned to other things. "Doug, this murder case seems like a tough one."

"Yeah. I'll be thinking about it in my sleep, going over little things I saw at the crime scene. Say, speaking of, can you get me a copy of the raw video Zeke shot? I'd like to check it out."

"No problem. Is there something that seems strange to you, Doug?"

"Yeah," he said, squeezing me tight before planting a kiss on my ear, "this conversation! We're supposed to be relaxing."

"Right, honey," I agreed momentarily as I locked his big ole *squeeze-me-tight* arms around my waist. "But I'm curious about something is all."

"Curiosity killed the cat."

"I don't think for a minute that you'd let anything happen to this cat."

"You know that's right. I want this cat alive and frisky so I can chase!"

Doug smooched me again and I was tickled. He was good for me: always forcing me to relax and making me laugh. We'd only been dating for a couple of months but the relationship was going well. The last thing I wanted to do was crush the mood, but I just had to ask a question about the case. It defied logic. I didn't want to ask it earlier because I didn't want to tip off my competition. "Say, Doug?"

"Hummpf?"

"Why move the body?"

"What?"

"The murdered John Doe at the pier. Why would the robber move the body there? If the criminal was familiar with the area—and there had to be some level of comfort, a comfort in knowledge because that's where the body was dumped—why there?"

Doug chuckled. "When I find the killer I'll conference you in on the questioning."

"But Doug—"

"Ssshhhhhh! We're here to relax and to support Jimmy, remember?"

"I know, I know. He's had it rough too. Doug, you can't even imagine."

"Oh yeah? Fill me in."

"Well, Jimmy's had some real up-and-down battles with cocaine."

"Ugh, drugs! That is a bona-fide can't-miss way to jack up your life."

"Say that, boy. And you know what? Peaches would drive me nuts calling me all hours of the night to vent about some mess Jimmy had gotten himself into. If he wasn't getting put out of his apartment or pawning his guitar, it was some crazy *exhale thang* with some old lady of his."

"Peaches has really stuck by him, huh?"

"Oh yeah. Peaches is like that. If she loves you, she'll back you up come hell or hurricane. And Peaches has always, kind of, well, idolized Jimmy."

"Why? Because of his talent?"

"Yeah that. And also because Jimmy never loses confidence in what he can do. When he's onstage, he owns it. Jimmy draws you to him. You just wanna hug the man to death. So if you think about it, Doug, that makes it easy to be confident."

"Other performers have to work at it."

"It took Peaches a long time to get her confidence together."

"No way. Seriously? Georgia, you've gotta be kidding. As much shit as Peaches can talk?"

"I know. But I'm telling you, Doug, Peaches used to get stage fright. It started when she first went solo. If her audience was good, Peaches was great. If the audience was funky or not warm, she'd start getting nervous and lose her edge."

"You wouldn't know it, not watching her do her thing now. Peaches is tight."

"Because Jimmy worked with her. He really took Peaches under his wing. Treated her like family. You know, my grandmother first saw Jimmy perform when he was a little boy back in the late fifties down South. Grandma says he was outside singing for pennies trying to buy food."

"How'd Jimmy get a break?"

"B.B. Watson," I said, taking a sip of my drink. "He discovered Jimmy when he was running the blues caravan. They used to barnstorm throughout the South. Couldn't play in the white clubs, so they'd set up tents by the railroad tracks and play their hearts out for tips."

"I think I read something about them in an article somewhere about legendary blues singers."

"That was in *Ebony*. My mom kept it because my grandmother sang with them for a while too. That's how we all got to know Jimmy. He's like family to us."

A drumroll from the stage drew Doug's attention. He beamed. "Here we go! Peaches is going to introduce Jimmy."

A waterfall of sweat was cascading down Peaches' face. She dabbed and fanned herself with a white hankie and then began the introduction. "This next performer is like family to me. Years ago, he helped me find my voice and develop my style. He has always been a good friend. But on top of being a friend he is the best guitarist I have ever heard."

"What about Johnny 'Guitar' Watson?' a patron yelled.

Peaches looked in that direction, then juked her neck like a bobble-head toy on a car dashboard. "What about him?"

Everyone laughed.

"This man is *thee best*, hear me? And tonight it is an honor and a pleasure to have him at my club after a long absence from the blues scene. I present to you none other than Mr. *Jim-may Flamingo!*"

Jimmy made a spirited entrance from a little spot off to the side in the wings. He walloped the strings with terrific energy when he played. Sometimes though, he'd play a sorrowful blues song, and use a technique he called cotton picking. The plucking was so quick that Jimmy's nimble left hand blurred but the sound seemed as if it would resonate inside your head forever.

Jimmy still had a conk. A conk is that fifties style that made a brother's hair look like asphalt: black, shiny, and hard. His skin was dark and his body thin; part of that was natural, but the unnatural ingestion of drugs had stripped his torso of what fat and muscle he had in no time flat.

Jimmy was recovering, happy to be sharing a gig with Peaches at the Blues Box. No one else wanted to give him a chance. Clean and sober he'd serenade the sun until it ran for cover at the end of the sky. But high? Jimmy would miss every gig and then have the nerve to get nasty when you interrupted his high to ask where he was.

Jimmy was called Flamingo because he had a long neck and when he jammed the guitar, he'd bob his head and stand with his feet flat, turned out like a bird braced to fly. When Jimmy performed he loved to wear vibrant jackets, colors that were a keen contrast to his sable skin and his ebony guitar.

Tonight, Jimmy was throwing down! I mean in the rarest of form. He walked the stage like a jilted lover walks the floor. The notes cried out from his guitar one minute and chuckled wryly the next. Somehow Jimmy cut off all space between himself and the audience. Felt like he was sitting in our laps, his head buried in our necks, pouring out his soul.

Just when Jimmy had you feeling the sorriest for him, he'd pump up the tempo with a new batch of songs he'd written. He'd lay the lyrics out like jewels for some lucky lady sitting close to the stage.

Jimmy turned up the heat by pulling out red roses, two dozen, he'd bought from a wholesale florist over on Cermak in Chinatown. He handed them out to various ladies until he was empty-handed and not a woman in the place was empty-hearted. Whether you were flowered or not, the manner in which Jimmy gave so freely made you feel immense joy.

Then Jimmy really got to work with that guitar of his. He played so hard and so well that we all screamed for him to stop, knowing dog-gone well we wanted more.

But could we stand it?

Could we stand it when Jimmy Flamingo dropped down on one knee? Could we stand it when he lay out on his back and sent a ghostly Hendrix riff sailing up to the ceiling?

We didn't know we could stand it till we stood it.

Jimmy played so tough our seats got hot. We couldn't sit down.
He loved the ovation. Jimmy clasped his hands together as if in
prayer and blessed the room with tears of joy.

The old Jimmy was back.

"Jim-may!" Doug welcomed him to our table with a hearty soul-
brother handshake. *"You are a bad-bad Negro.* Waitress! A round
here right away."

I started bawling Jimmy out quick; I mean *on ya mark, set, go!*
"Man, you can't come into my sister's place and upstage her. Is this
just an opening-night thing or do you plan on leaving your manners
at the coat check every night?"

"Every night, Georgia."

"Good. Then me and Doug will definitely be back."

At that moment Peaches came hobbling over to the table, wrapping her cushy arms around Jimmy. "You let it all hang out tonight,
baby. I mean you left your drawers on the doorknob. Wasn't he
great, y'all?"

We all agreed and Peaches gave me a big hug then gave Doug a big
smooch on the lips. "Watch it, Hot Mama," I signified. "Don't take
share and share alike too far." I pointed down. "And why do you
have on my shoes!"

"As many pairs of shoes as you have?" Peaches said, and gave me
a smack with her hips as she took a seat. "You know every shoe
designer on the planet. You won't even miss these bad boys, probably bought 'em eons ago."

"So?"

"So—you have the best taste and the most money, whoop, there
it is!"

"Peaches, I gave you the keys to my place in case there happened
to be an emergency. I did not give you the keys so you could go
Goodwill shopping among my stuff. I haven't had those shoes on
myself yet."

Peaches kicked off one of the pumps and began rubbing her toes, "You ought to be glad too. You know these damn shoes are too small. Got me walking around like a peg-leg whore. What's up with these nines? You know we wear a ten."

"Hey, big-footed woman!" Jimmy cracked then mimicked a guitar riff with tight jaws. "*Whammh-whammh-wah-wah!* Big-footed woman, *whammh-whammh-wah-wah!*"

Now see, don't take me there. "Curtail that nonsense, Mr. Flamingo. And for the record, I do wear a nine."

Peaches swiveled her neck. "Whatever! I'm just glad to see Jimmy back. He was kind of depressed the last couple of days. Had me worried there for a minute."

"Forget that," Jimmy said with a smile. "Between Peaches and some of my old partners coming over to my place—I got the wake-up call I needed. Made me believe in myself again. All my blues are dead and gone—except the ones I pluck out of my guitar."

"I'll toast to that!" Doug said, pouring the champagne. Jimmy grabbed a glass with his left hand and held it up next to Doug's. The rest of us joined in on the toast. Who knew that this would be the last good time we'd have together for quite a while? Things were about to get tense and ugly for all of us.

Chapter Three

I WAS IN THE NEWSROOM EARLY TUESDAY MORNING, MAKING a dub tape for Doug. I was settling comfortably into one of two padded chairs, rewinding the video that Zeke had shot at Manning Pier the day before. The loud swish of Beta tape rewinding filled the tiny edit bay I was working in.

An edit bay at WJIV is enclosed in glass, with patio doors, also glass, soundproofed, with a desk, Sony edit equipment that includes a fancy computer, and three television monitors. I watched the video closely.

Tight shot. The victim's face. Placid. Alarming in its stillness. A diver's hand white from the cold water helped to lift the back of the head as the land crew hauled the body out of Lake Michigan. Water that appeared blue in the bed of the lake dripped a thin root-beer brown as it stripped itself away from the victim's body.

The door of the edit bay slid open. "Whatcha doing?"

It was my friend Clarice, a researcher at WJIV—Channel 8. She had a cigarette dangling from her hand and blew smoke over both our heads as she stood behind me. Sitting, I was almost as tall as she was standing, but the sister is nitty-gritty. *Clarice don't play, baby.*

"Hey, Clarice. I'm cuing up this video to make a dub for Doug. He wants to see it; might help with the murder case."

"Sho-nuff must be love," Clarice sang. She has a rusty voice that leaps from her mouth. "Doing favors for the honey, huh?"

"Get out of my business, okay, Miss Nosy Rosy?"

Then I saw it.

I slammed my palm down on the rewind knob. That stopped the video cold. Then I used my index finger to shuttle backward, frame by frame, so the video looked like the slow blink of an eye. Zeke's shot was panning from the victim's head to his feet, and there at the feet, something caught my eye. The shoes.

"Clarice, look at this."

"What?"

"Those shoes . . . the leather, the design, they're expensive."

"So? He wasn't murdered for having bad taste."

"No. Those are very expensive shoes, I think I know that make."

"I believe it," Clarice said, taking another puff of her cigarette, "the way you love shoes."

I strained to see the logo and said out loud, "What are they?"

"Bruno Magli," Clarice snorted.

"Please, no O.J. jokes."

"Well, Georgia, you can't possibly be asking me, could you?" Clarice said even though she had begun scrutinizing the video too. She stomped her feet one at a time: "Sears. Roebuck."

I laughed.

"Wait, Georgia. Right there. It's fuzzy but on the bottom of the shoes, there's an engraving. I can't read it."

"I see it. I'll get the art department to blow it up. I'm telling you, I know that shoe style."

I popped the tape out of the machine and carried it over to the art department.

Every newsroom has an art department. They're the graphic specialists. They're responsible for visual effects that help to illustrate a story when there's no video or when producers and reporters want to fancy up a broadcast. The colorful maps used are made by the graphic artists. The pictures of murder victims framed against a solid colored background with their name on it: the graphic folks do that too. They are very creative and very underpaid.

"Hey, Kyle," I said, rushing into the art department area, which was down the hall from the edit bays and the main newsroom. The hallway was narrow and the lights dimmed to the absolute lowest. Framed prints and Broadway posters lined the walls. Hip rock music hummed in the air. Kyle, with his chic turtleneck and black jeans, sat at his computer working on a series of graphics that illustrated how blood flows through the heart.

"Hi, Georgia," he said without turning around. Kyle had a firm grasp on the computer wand. He flicked and dabbed at an electronic board to paste in color and add definition.

"Kyle, I need a big favor."

Expressionless, Kyle began to whistle about two bars of "America the Beautiful"; stopping abruptly, scowling, he said, "As in this minute?"

I nodded yes and tried to look pitiful.

"Huh," Kyle grunted, leaving his mouth slightly ajar, his tongue flush against the roof of his mouth. He slowly shook his head no and his heavy mop of black hair danced on top of his head.

"C'mon, Kyle. You can squeeze in this *little bitty old easy-pleasy* job for me. I know you can."

"Georgia, they're killing me as it is. I'm working on the medical segment for the early show. There's a new procedure being tested for bypass surgery. Each step has to be illustrated by a new graphic. This is page four and there are four more to go."

Kyle looked at his watch, a silver Mickey Mouse timepiece left over from his ABC/Disney days.

I held a hopeful breath.

"Come back in an hour, maybe." He laughed in a tone that let me know the dude was super-serious.

"Kyle, I'm working that murdered John Doe case at Manning Pier."

"I was off yesterday, but I caught your live shot. You must have almost wet your pants out there!"

"Bet my interview Erin did, the way she shot up out of that water. I've got the raw video from the scene."

Kyle whistled more of "America the Beautiful."

Like that was going to stop me from begging? Please. "Check this out. There's this shot on the tape that might be a clue. It has to do with the victim's shoes."

Then between the purple mountains and the fruited plain I lied my ass off.

"I ran into Fay in the hallway." Fay was the other graphic artist. "And she said that there is no way to clean up the video and see a clear shot of the shoes."

Kyle stopped whistling and stopped working too. He leaned back in the chair, swiveled in my direction, crossed his legs at the ankles, and looked at me. His eyes twinkled and sparkled. A mischievous smile crossed his lips.

I shrugged and looked as helpless as I possibly could. "What?"

Kyle rubbed his chin and then said softly, "We both know that if Fay wasn't the boss's squeeze, she wouldn't even have a job. If you gave her a box of crayons and a picture of a square, she wouldn't be able to stay inside the lines."

I was counting on his dislike of Fay to work to my advantage. But I didn't want to completely use Kyle. He's a good guy. "If you try for ten minutes and you can't get it, I'll go. If you nail it, all the better. Either way, I'm treating you to lunch. Deal?"

Kyle cracked his knuckles before whirling his hand in a magician's motion. "The tape, please!"

Like Kool and the Gang sings, "Get Down on It!" I watched as Kyle popped the tape into a Beta deck and looked at the fuzzy image as it slowly filled the computer screen.

"Kyle, it clears up just a few frames forward."

He nodded, concentrating.

"Freeze!"

Kyle stopped. Then he began the work of Merlin. He tweaked and enhanced, blowing up the picture, working frame by frame. "You said ten minutes, huh?"

I was startled, then realized he was chuckling under his breath. "Don't tease me. Help a sister out."

At that moment, I recognized it. The seal and the shape of the heel that I hadn't completely pegged before, the unique slant mark used both on the men's and the women's shoes. I read the engraving on the sole.

"Martelli—twelve triple E," I shouted.

"Yep," Kyle said, "and Martelli's ain't cheap. I was killing time at lunch one day and stopped in the Michigan Avenue store. Wasn't a shoe in there under three hundred dollars."

"My ex-boyfriend Max loved those shoes. The old guy custom-makes some of the shoes, one of the few people in the country who still believes in the art of shoemaking. Sews parts of the sole by hand. How many customers could he have that wear a twelve triple E that fit the murder victim's description?"

"Not many, I would imagine."

"Can you give me a freeze frame of that shot and run it through the Polaroid so I can have a snapshot of the shoes. Oh, I'll need the victim's face too. There's a shot at the end of the tape that's very clean."

"Big lunch did you say?"

"Oh yeah. Big Mac, super-sized."

Kyle jerked around.

"I'm joking!" Then I pulled out a twenty-dollar bill.

Kyle took the money then quickly began working on my Polaroids. I would take them and dump the tape off with Clarice, who would get it dubbed and send it by courier to Doug at the cop shop.

I huddled with the producer of the noon show. I told him that I had a feeling in my bones. And my bones don't jones for nothing. I wanted a cameraman to follow a hot lead but the next cameraman wasn't due in for another hour! Think I was waiting? Think again! They'd have to just meet me there because I was jonesing for an exclusive, to identify the murder victim before anyone from the competing stations did.

I would too.

But I would also get more than I bargained for.

Chapter Four

CHICAGO'S NORTH MICHIGAN AVENUE: A STRETCH OF STORES and salons that rival Beverly Hills' Rodeo Drive. Imagine that kind of chic with a warmer, less pretentious Midwest feel.

Restaurants serve Old World cuisine in lavish venues of contemporary design. The specialty shops have windows filled with malnourished mannequins clothed in outfits from Paris runways. Sometimes, in the summer, the sidewalks are lined with commissioned pieces of art from local talent.

Mother Winter seemed to be in the middle of a hot flash. It was nearly fifty degrees. I was loving it; as a matter of fact all of Chicago was loving it. The streets were packed with people strolling, shopping, some workers stealing a hooky moment. The workers stood out in their ankle socks and sneakers, out of sync with their otherwise very businesslike attire. Most of them were clothes-shopping.

I was shopping too—for clues to the identity of a murdered man.

Martelli's was the least haughty-looking store on the block; the window was frosted in silver with the store name printed in small, block script across the top. In the bottom corner of the glass front door was a sign that said, "CLOSED DUE TO WINTER FASHION SHOW."

Like that was gonna keep Georgia Barnett out! I banged on the door.

A pudgy man came to the front of the store. He had stringy,

bleached-blond hair slicked straight back. His baby face didn't seem to fit with his middle-aged body. He stared blankly in my direction long enough for me to take a deep breath and release it with a sigh. Then the clerk rumpled his brow and his nose twitched slightly just as he began to wave a cautionary index finger at me, saying, "Closed!"

My right hand flew up to my ear, "What? What's that?"

The clerk had on a dark blue jacket, white turtleneck, and khaki pants. He whipped back the jacket with his hands, planting them on his sloping hips, shaking his head.

I shrugged my shoulders, put my hand on the doorknob, flicked my wrist twice, and listened to the lock grunt.

I watched the clerk's chest heave as he flicked the latch on his side and swung the door open.

"Miss, can't you see that we're closed. Now would you please—"

"Is Mr. Martelli in?"

"Yes, but he cannot be disturbed. He's in seclusion selecting stock for a special Winter Fashion Show at the Merchandise Mart."

I stuck one of my size tens in the door. Yeah, yeah y'all . . . Peaches wasn't tellin' no story.

"Sir," I said, "he'll probably want to see me."

"I don't think so!" The top of his head was level with my chest. He smelled Chanel. And acted like I didn't. "Now, if you'll excuse me, miss."

My size-ten shoe was the doorstop that kept him from abruptly ending our conversation. I rushed my words. "Do you think Mr. Martelli would come out of his creative shell to talk to a television reporter?"

The wall of seclusion melted faster than snow off a pair of boots sitting by a radiator. The clerk's pale face flowered rose. "Oh, what channel?"

"Eight. I'm Georgia Barnett."

"Oh no!" he said with a grin, revealing big, straight white teeth. The clerk buttoned his jacket and said, "I'm sorry. I didn't recognize you. I'm so sorry."

"No problem."

"Can I be in the story?" He became giggly. "I can show you around. I'd love to be on TV. Is this about the hot fashions this Christmas season?"

"No. It's about a murder and I don't think you want to be part of that kind of a story."

His blue eyes doubled in size. "You're kidding! That's horrible."

I glanced over the clerk's right shoulder to the rear. I saw a double mahogany door with a sign that read "STOCK."

I began walking. "There, I presume," and I showed myself in, leaving the flustered clerk where he stood.

"Mr. Martelli?" I called, surprised at the vastness of the space. There were wooden slats that resembled library bookcases, reaching nearly ten feet high, each cut with a shelving bed that holds a pair of shoes at an angle, all lining the west wall. Then there were tons of equipment—even a few 1950s black, wrought-iron sewing machines mixed in with the super-duper jobs of the new millennium.

I knew Bre Martelli when I saw him. I'd seen feature articles on his business in the *Chicago Sun-Times* and in the *Chicago Tribune*. Pictures of him had been center stage on the society pages as well. Charity functions. Exhibit openings. College scholarships. Dude had style and banged together some mean pairs of kicks.

"Young woman," a voice chided from my left rear. It was an ample sound peppered with a European accent. "What are you doing back here?"

I turned.

Mr. Martelli was standing there with a rag, wiping what looked like boot black off his palms. His eyebrows were untamed, hovering together like weeds. His hair was long, crinkly, and airborne with static cling. The creases of his face had the rugged but still appealing look of a well-traveled shoe. "Mr. Martelli, I'm Georgia Barnett, Channel 8 News."

"Of course I recognize you, lovely lady!" Mr. Martelli stuffed the soiled rag into the back pocket of his worn slacks. "Excuse my work clothes," he said, tugging at the bottom of his ill-fitting black sweater. "To what do I owe the pleasure of this visit?"

"I wish it was to buy a pair of your wonderful shoes, Mr. Martelli. But I'm afraid it's not."

"Sounds serious, young lady."

"It is. Did you happen to hear about the dead body that turned up at Manning Pier yesterday?"

"I'm afraid I missed the news yesterday. And I haven't had time to look at the paper today." Mr. Martelli straightened out the rumpled sleeves of his sweater. "But what does all that have to do with me?"

I pulled the Polaroid of the shoes out of my pocket first.

Take it easy, I thought, *real easy. You never want to rattle a potential interview; people will clam up on you.*

Mr. Martelli slowly took hold of the picture. His hand was scarred from years of sewing and felt gritty to the touch. A pair of round specs hung on a chain about his neck. Mr. Martelli took them, shook out the metal arms, and put them on, holding the Polaroid at an angle in the dim overhead light. He clucked his tongue before taking a deep breath. Mr. Martelli exhaled and thumped the corner of the snapshot with his finger, speaking firmly. "Yes, those are my shoes."

"I thought so. It's a size . . ."

"Twelve triple E; I see clearly with my glasses."

Now for the next step, I thought. I don't want to startle him, or upset him so much that he can't help. "Mr. Martelli. The man wearing those shoes is the murder victim."

His mouth released two grinding breaths as his lungs double-clutched inside his chest. Behind Mr. Martelli's button black eyes, there was some sense of knowing.

"The victim is a white male, sixty to sixty-five years old, five nine, muscular build—one hundred seventy pounds. Gray hair. Brown eyes. Does that description sound familiar to you?"

Mr. Martelli thought for a moment, "I don't know," he said. He looked at the shoes again. "Murder, my God."

There were two brown folding chairs in the corner next to a rack holding three pairs of heelless boots. I took Mr. Martelli by the elbow, turned him in that direction. "Let's sit down over here."

This man, old enough to be my father, went without question like a little boy. "I know this is very hard, Mr. Martelli." We sat. "Think. You have a very selective clientele. Does that description fit any of your customers?"

"Yes." Mr. Martelli grimaced. "Two, maybe three gentlemen." Then he swallowed hard before he nudged his glasses back up on the bridge of his nose. "I don't know. I never had to deal with anything like this before."

"Of the customers that come to mind, who wore a size twelve triple E?"

Mr. Martelli thought hard. Then I saw something in his eyes. "You think you know who it is?"

I had another Polaroid in my pocket. It was a shot of the dead man's face.

"I have another snapshot in my pocket, Mr. Martelli. But this is a picture of the victim. It's not grisly. It's not gruesome. But it is a dead person: a person that I believe you know. Can you look at the picture and tell me if you can positively identify him?"

Mr. Martelli swallowed hard again but did not speak.

"You wouldn't just be helping me, you'd be helping the police too. Please, we don't know who this victim is yet. His family hasn't even been notified."

"Of course." Mr. Martelli sighed. "Whatever I can do."

I showed him the Polaroid. Sadness quickly filled his eyes. Mr. Martelli spoke deliberately, calmly. "This man has had an account here for more than ten years."

"Who is he?"

"His name is Fab Weaver. He's a good customer. I can't believe he was murdered. What happened?"

"Someone shot him to death and dumped his body at Manning Pier."

"But why? Do the police know who did it?"

"No. So far they don't have any suspects. He hasn't been officially identified yet. If it weren't for your shoes, Mr. Martelli, their distinctiveness, I wouldn't have been able to figure it out myself."

"Fab Weaver was a good man, a nice man. Why would anyone want to hurt him?"

"It looks like a robbery so far. His wallet was gone. No jewelry. Listen, do you have a current address for him?"

"Yes, just let me check my files . . . please follow me."

Mr. Martelli headed toward a rear staircase leading to a large office on the fourth floor.

I continued to fire off questions while jotting everything down in my reporter's notepad. "Do you know if the victim had any family? What he did for a living?"

"Fab Weaver did something in real estate. Owned some rental properties. Never mentioned a wife, but he did have at least one child—a grown son. I know that for sure. He's a nasty little son of a gun."

"What makes you say that?" I asked as we entered the office. It was a bit cluttered but had a large window with a view of cars bustling down Lake Shore Drive where the road curled around the water.

"Well, Fab Weaver came in once for a fitting, for a boot. That man loved boots. Have a seat, Miss Barnett, please, while I find the information."

"Georgia, please. Call me Georgia."

Mr. Martelli smiled. "Thank you. While Fab Weaver was here, his son came in looking for him. The kid was yelling and screaming."

"About what?"

"Nothing that I could make total sense of. Had something to do with money, I got that much. It was a lot of rambling. Cursing."

"Did they fight? Get physical or anything?"

"No, Weaver just looked at his son like he was out of his mind. The boy had no honor for his father. Had he been a boy of mine, I would have closed that disrespectful mouth."

"Yeah, you and me both."

"How do the young people say it now?" Mr. Martelli asked. "I'm *Old World.*"

I had to laugh at the man. "You mean *old school.*"

"That's it." Mr. Martelli smiled, relaxing a bit. "I threatened to call the police. That made him leave. He seemed high on something. I remember Weaver mumbled something about drugs and the kid hating him."

"So you think Fab Weaver's son is a heavy user?"

"Could be. The way he acted that day. But Weaver never said any more about it. He looked very upset, almost fearful. Ahhh, here it is!"

Mr. Martelli pulled out a credit sheet with Fab Weaver's account information on it.

"Great."

I'd broken the story by identifying the victim. My late crew would be here any minute and then I would interview Mr. Martelli on camera about the victim. He'd say what he'd already told me about Fab Weaver being a good guy and a good customer.

But in TV news you have to be sure. The name of the game is fast and factual. You can't be in such a hurry to scoop that you make a mistake. People at your station and people at the competition will rag on you for centuries. And that ain't nothing nice.

I was excited! The dead man had a name. But I needed someone else to confirm it too. Mr. Martelli gave me Fab Weaver's home address. I knew I should probably call the police and have them call the family; but I couldn't chance losing my scoop. I checked my watch. I'd have enough time to get to Fab Weaver's house before my story was due.

Fab Weaver's house. That was my next stop. I wondered would I run into his son? I didn't like him already. But once he learned of his father's death, surely he would be devastated. I wondered, what was between them? What would make Fab Weaver think his own son hated him?

Chapter Five

HEY, GEORGIA," ZEKE HOLLERED, "WATCH ME TAKE THIS turn without hitting the brake."

"Wait!" I shouted.

Doggone it, too late.

I watched Zeke hunch his body over the steering wheel, elbows out. His facial hairs were dying to do their own thing. They were pointy and unruly, sprouting every which-ah-way all around his chin, the beginnings of a scruffy beard. Zeke made race-car sounds with his mouth.

The boy loves to irritate me with those speed-racer antics—can't stop him and can't talk him out of it. And I just know his Southern mama taught him better. I winced as that corner got bigger and badder, faster and sooner than it certainly should have. We turned and I swear it felt like I was seven years old again on the carnival Tilt-a-Whirl ride.

"Wheeww!" Zeke cheered, then grinned at me. "Am I not the best driver on the planet, huh? Just say it."

"Boy, you do that again and I'm gonna beat your butt."

"Scaredy cat!" Zeke poked me in the side with his index finger. "Best reporter in town and afraid of a little speed."

Luckily for Zeke we were pulling up in front of Fab Weaver's house. It was a large double-lot frame house, white and teal in color. It had a front porch with thick, colonial posts. We were in Lincoln Park, an upscale neighborhood on the North Side of Chicago. Old money and "young up-and-comers" lived here, predominantly white, very little black and nare a speck of brown. No tweeners—working class, lower middle class—just *the very moneyed and the trying-to-be.*

Fab Weaver must have been kicking butt in real estate to afford to live here. This house was worth, with the double lot, about a million dollars. *Easy-pleasy.* I peered around the back. Eyeballed a three-car garage, spanking new. A gigantic oak tree was centered in the yard. It was naked, but not a leaf could be seen on the browned lawn. Every inch of the exterior was well kept.

Zeke followed me up to the door. His camera was loaded and ready to fire up, but anchored to his shoulder, not on. I waited until I got flush right of the door but at an angle so that I couldn't be completely viewed from the window. Zeke stood kitty-corner to the door.

"I'm hot," he said, turning the camera on and setting up a shot that framed me right and kept the door center.

I rang the bell. And waited. After a minute, a woman answered, "Yes?"

She was about forty to forty-five years old, white with a spicy complexion, slim build, dark hair combed back in a ponytail. She was a pretty woman, green eyes, a full nose, high cheekbones. There was a warmth about her. She held a dust cloth in her hand and she wore a loose T-shirt and jeans with black sneakers.

Was this woman the victim's wife? I trod lightly.

"Hi. Are you Mrs. Fab Weaver?"

"No," she said, "I'm the cleaning lady. Can I help you?"

"Yes. I'm Georgia Barnett, Channel 8 News."

Zeke stepped into view, filming.

"Wait a minute. What's going on?"

"We're looking for Mrs. Fab Weaver or another family member."

"There is no Mrs. Weaver. I don't know how to reach anybody in Mr. Weaver's family. I don't know what else to tell you. No one's here but me."

"I'd like to talk to you then if I could. Can we come in?"

"I don't know. What's this about?"

"We have some very important news. And it would be difficult to go into it talking through a doorway. Please, can we come in, just for a few minutes?"

"I guess . . ." the cleaning lady said, her body tensing.

"Thank you . . . ummmm," I said, fishing for her name.

"Angelina."

I followed Angelina into the house. We turned left and headed into the living room. The hardwood floors had a glistening polish to them. There were a few pieces of elegant furniture. The walls were painted a rust color then trimmed with floral print borders; the impersonal air of the room screamed paid interior decorator.

I sat down on the couch. Angelina sat down next to me and began snapping the dust cloth in her hands. A small puff of dirt floated into the air. Zeke was still standing.

"Angelina," I said, "I have bad news. A body was discovered at Manning Pier yesterday and we have reason to believe it's Mr. Weaver."

She gasped. "What?" A nervous twitch settled beneath her eyes. Angelina licked her lips once. "I don't believe it!"

"I have in my pocket a photo of the victim. An acquaintance says it's Fab Weaver, but I need to be absolutely sure. I need double verification. Can you take a look at the picture and tell me whether or not it's Mr. Weaver?"

"I don't know if I wanna do that, get so involved like that."

Angelina was stuck. When you're working a story, a news story in a big city, sometimes people come up and beg to tell you anything they *know* and *don't know*, just so they can be on TV. Fifteen minutes of fame in TV news is only a fifteen-second sound bite. Some people are dying just to get that.

Then there are the other folks.

Angelina appeared to be part of that posse. I'm talking about the folks who are leery to get involved, to be helpful in solving a crime or providing information for a news story. They're stuck on the *Should I?* ledge. To do my job right, I have to lure them off that ledge onto solid *I need to* ground.

"Angelina, I know what I'm asking is not easy. You're probably thinking something like, Hey, she deals with this kindah stuff all the time so it's no big deal for her. I'm not getting involved."

An olive blush slowly made its way across Angelina's face; her fingers flexed, and her eyes seemed to agree with my assessment.

"But people have to get involved. Think. If this was a person in your family, wouldn't you want someone to help?"

Angelina sighed, then sat up on the edge of the couch. She thought for several moments. Had I won her over? I wasn't sure but I was definitely going to keep pushing.

"Just take a look, that's all."

I held out the Polaroid I'd shown Mr. Martelli and timidly Angelina took it. Slowly she nodded the affirmative, before whispering, "That's him, yes. What happened?"

"He was shot to death, his body dumped in Lake Michigan."

Angelina shook her head, speechless.

"I'd like to talk to you very quickly if I could about Mr. Weaver. About working for him. Anything you might know about him and his family."

Angelina stood up. "I don't really know anything. Maybe you should talk to somebody else."

I took her hand and held it firmly, but gently. "You've been great so far. I just want to ask you some questions about what kind of a boss he was. Very simple stuff. Just relax."

Angelina sat back down.

Zeke stopped shooting. He headed back out to the truck to get a tripod.

"Angelina, I know hearing this kind of news can really shake a person up. Even someone like me."

Angelina raised a cynical eyebrow, "You?"

I couldn't help but laugh a little bit. "Yes, me. Think about it. At one time or another every veteran reporter was a kid on the job. It's tough for you to go on camera . . . now imagine how I feel asking the questions."

"I guess it would be hard."

"You better believe it. I tell you, the truth it can be a hardship. I remember the first time I covered a story about a murder victim. I was working in a little town in Ohio. I sat in the truck, trying to get up the nerve to go knocking on doors to talk to the victim's neighbors."

"Took a while to get up your nerve?"

"I must've sat there, maybe, close to forty minutes. Then I just did it. I told myself I had to do my job because it was important; but it was more important to make these people feel at ease, because I knew it was tough on everybody. So I just want you to relax, to know I understand. We can do this thing together."

Zeke came back in. He put the camera on the sticks and framed a shot of Angelina and me on the couch. Zeke gave me the go-ahead.

"This is just routine, so don't be nervous. Can you please say and spell your first and last name for editing purposes?"

"Angelina Rosseni, A-n-g-e-l-i-n-a R-o-s-s-e-n-i."

I had my reporter's notepad out, flipped to a clean page. I had questions ready to go. I waited until I felt she was stable, breathing easier; then I would scribble notes while maintaining as much eye contact as I could.

"How long have you worked for Mr. Weaver?"

"A little over a year."

"Was he a good employer, even-tempered, paid you well . . .?"

"Yes, Mr. Weaver is very nice. I came in weekly to do light cleaning and cooking. Always paid on time, his attorney mailed me my check."

"Do you know the attorney's name?"

"No, not by heart. I'd have to check one of my pay stubs at home for it."

"Can you find that after we're through? I'll give you a number where you can reach me with it later."

"Sure."

"Good. Angelina, you said at the door that there is no Mrs. Weaver. Is he divorced or widowed?"

"Widowed."

"Recently?"

"No, when I started working here, Mr. Weaver said then that his wife had died a while back."

"What about children? I know he has a son. Do you know how we can get in contact with him?"

"I never met his son. I heard Mr. Weaver talking to him on the phone a couple of times briefly, but that's it."

"What's his son's name?"

"Guy. Guy Weaver."

"The times that you overheard their conversation, how did it sound? Strained? Angry?"

"No. Just normal."

"No arguing or anything, Angelina?"

"No."

"Do you know the name of Mr. Weaver's real estate business?"

"Real estate?"

"Yes, we have information that he got his money from real estate."

"No. I mean he may own property, I don't know anything about that."

"Hey," Zeke said, interrupting the interview, something he seldom did. "Are those gold records on the wall in that other room there? I can see them in the shot."

I turned and looked and through the open door, into the hallway, a second door was ajar, Zeke wasn't kidding: there were gold records on the wall! "Fab Weaver was in the record business?"

"Yeah, a long time ago."

"Can we take a look?"

Angelina got up. Zeke backpedaled and angled for the doorway. He wanted to get a shot of us walking out of the room together. We walked and I made small talk with her for video purposes.

Once inside the study, I was amazed! On one wall there were five gold records. I'm not jiving. A line of gold records! Then on the opposite wall, there were photos of groups from the sixties, all black groups and singers. Head shots they're called in the business. I remember helping Peaches pick out one of hers to send to an ad agency that was looking to hire a blues singer for a beer commercial.

This room was fantastic. It looked like somebody had ripped off the lobby of Soul Train. And it brought back a deluge of memories for me as well.

Music runs in my family. It started with my grandmother and flowed on down to Peaches and me. Seeing all those old photos made me think about some of the old songstresses who used to hang out in my grandmother's basement back in the late sixties/early seventies. Peaches and me weren't nothing but little old chocolate chips back then.

It would be late on a Friday night; no school and no church the next day. The basement had couches on both sides of the room plus some folding chairs too. Grandma set it up like a stage, with the center of the room uncluttered and open. In the corner was a black, upright Lyon-Healy piano, white keys yellowed with age but in perfect tune.

The record player was in the other corner. It had a nickel on the needle held by a rubber band to keep it from skipping 'cross the forty-fives and the thirty-threes that were being played.

A raggedy amp, donated by an old bass player who was sweet on my grandmother, was in the back of the room. It had a plug-in mike and a long cord. The music would be playing and the songstresses would sit around eating potluck, and what luck it was—mustard greens, pinto beans, hot-water corn bread, gumbo, cornbeef and cabbage, fried chicken, pig's feet, potato salad, coleslaw, blackberry cobbler, pound cake, and a package of store-bought doughnuts from some cheap sucker trying to get over.

Neighbors would come over to hear the women sing, mostly the blues and some gospel. They would grab that mike and cut loose; sweat would get to popping and those boogie-butter hips would get to rolling. The songstresses were all getting up in age and would have hot flashes and flashbacks at the same time.

They'd fan with old playbills—the photos of their young faces fluttering back at them like slivers from a broken mirror. They'd reminisce about the old clubs in Chicago that had gotten torn down, about how fabulous they were. Sparkly clothes. Short pay. Long nights. Roof-raising cheers.

They grumped lovingly about how their throats scorched and only a squirt of honey could put out the fire; about who couldn't sing but made it and who could sing but didn't.

Then my grandma and those songstresses would get that mike and belt out a little *something-something*. No band backed them up anymore. No manager stood in the wings to take a huge cut of their pay, leaving their pocketbooks damn near empty. It was just us. The folks from the neighborhood trying to give them a heyday flashback and all the love we could muster.

Some of Grandma's friends would pose like the players I was looking at now on Fab Weaver's wall. Much 'tude and authority were being given off. Hips out, heads back, chests up, and even though they didn't have on their tight sparkly clothes like in the photo album being circulated at the time, they still looked like the stars they were. Especially here in Chicago; the blues mecca of the colored world as the old folks called Record Row.

"Hey, Georgia," Zeke said, "you with us or somewhere else?"

I threw a quick smile over my shoulder at Zeke and Angelina. "I'm here. This is impressive. Where's Weaver?"

"This photo here." Angelina pointed to the top left-hand corner of the wall. "That's Mr. Weaver when he was young in front of the record company he owned."

Zeke stood flat-footed, then zoomed in on the photos. I popped up on my tiptoes. I saw a Michigan Avenue street sign behind a group of baby-faced black teenage boys, all dolled up in tight blue silk suits with skinny ties. Looking like the Temps and, I'm sure, praying to be that successful. Two of the group members were kneeling, holding a sign that said THE FOUR LOCOMOTIONS.

Fab Weaver was leaning on one of the teens' shoulders, grinning like he was fit to be tied. He was a stark contrast to his post-mortem self, I swear. He was young, dark-haired, muscular, stocky, with a rough look about him, cut from Sly Stallone cloth. He was on the verge of being fine, but only managing kinda cute.

On Fab Weaver's desk, next to the wall, was a scrapbook. I opened it and began flipping through the pages. Zeke was standing behind me now, focusing. "Turn slow."

I gradually flipped the pages one at a time so that we would have

extra video. I eyeballed the headlines that fluttered past. FAB WEAVER
HOT NEW PRODUCER. FAB WEAVER DISCOVERS THE FOUR LOCOMOTIONS.
FAB WEAVER PENS ANOTHER HIT.

Angelina was now standing behind Zeke and me. I turned toward
her. Zeke focused us together in a two-shot. "Angelina, when was
the last time you saw Fab Weaver?"

Her eyes suddenly got shifty, "Umh, about three days ago, Saturday afternoon."

I made a mental note. So he was murdered sometime between
Saturday afternoon and Monday afternoon when his body washed
up during my live shot. That's a forty-eight-hour window of opportunity.

"Was he acting funny, strange? Upset?"

"I really don't think I should say, I don't . . ."

Girlfriend got awful nervous. Awful quick. I began to bum-rush
her with the facts. "Listen, in a murder case any little thing can be
important. Angelina, you would only be helping the investigation."

"But I don't want to put myself in danger."

"Why would you be in any danger?"

Angelina couldn't have been any quieter if she was one of Bay-
bay's kids and I had asked her, Who broke that?

"Listen to me, Angelina. If you don't want to tell me, at the
very least you need to tell the police. It might help them find the
killer."

"I—I don't know if I can trust them; maybe what I know would
help, but I—I'm afraid. It's just that sometimes the police seem so
uncaring. They don't give a damn about you."

"Listen," I said, putting my arm around her shoulder. "I understand that you feel apprehensive. But I know someone you can trust.
I know someone who will be fair and who won't leave you hanging if
there's any trouble. Let me call him for you."

"I don't know." She looked down nervously, then up at Zeke. "Hey, mister, no more filming."

Zeke glanced at me and kept right on filming.

"Zeke, stop. We don't want her to be uncomfortable. Just wait." He turned off the camera.

"Angelina, listen to me for a second. We can disguise your face, change the sound of your voice. You can talk on camera and no one will be able to tell it's you. I won't identify you."

"No! No—no more filming."

"If you don't talk to us, talk to the police. You'll regret it if you don't. You're upset. Someone you know has been killed, that's totally understandable. But you have to talk to the police."

Angelina stood there thinking. "All right," she said after a couple of minutes, "make the call." Then she sighed. "I'm dying for some coffee, you guys want some?"

"Best idea I've heard all morning." Zeke smiled. "Thank you."

Angelina left the room.

I took out my cell phone and called Doug's pager number. We had a little code. Seven-one-one: Watch the show. I called sometimes when I had a big story and I wanted an honest opinion on how well I did. Four-one-one: Date's off, will call later. We were wearing that one out! He'd get stuck on a case or I'd get sent out to chase a breaking story. And of course, nine-one-one: Emergency. That meant call me back quick.

I paged Doug and put in 911.

"What's up, Georgia?"

"A bunch. Where are you?"

"At the station."

"Okay, one: Watch my live shot and package at noon. It'll be on in less than an hour. I've not only identified the murder victim but I've got someone who may have some information that will give you a

break in the case. So two: After you watch my lead story I'll page you
with the address so you can get right over here."

"Where's here?" Doug asked.

"The victim's house."

"Yeah, sister sleuth, you are on fire today. Give me the address
now."

"No, baby. I know you like to let the desk sarge know where you
are—I can dig that. But he might leak it to the competition and I'm
not about to lose my exclusive after busting my tail-feather all the
live-long day."

"All right, no need to fight about it. I'll see you soon."

We hung up.

Angelina came back with a tray, cups, and coffee. She sipped,
staring out the window. I sipped and worked on my story.

The reporter's written part of the story is called the track.

When you take quotes from the people you've interviewed and
insert them in between the tracks, those are called sound bites.

The pictures that cover the written words, the track, is called
background video or b-roll.

I like to write while I'm being driven from one location to
another. I think about how I'm going to write a story while I'm
interviewing someone. It's second nature to me now. See, a reporter
has to sift through a bunch of facts. In television news, you have to
boil those facts down to what works best with the pictures in order to
tell the most complete and engaging story.

You have what's called a hit time. That's the exact minute—down
to the second—when the story airs in the show. If you miss your hit
time, you are in big trouble! I had to hustle to make the hit time for
my live shot and package.

And the time allotted for all of that is very limited. A package
usually runs anywhere from one minute to two minutes in length.

Today's special: Murder Update.

Right after my story aired, I gave Doug Fab Weaver's address. Then my cell phone rang. It was Clarice.

"Slamming!" she howled into the receiver. "No one else had anything new on the story. Bing was standing here, and girl, I swear he was so happy, I thought he was gonna grab himself!"

I laughed. Bing is boss hog. That means he's the news director and he is a sho' nuff tough taskmaster.

Zeke heard me talking on the phone and started dipping in my conversation, "What, Georgia? What now?"

I had to tease him. "Is this your dime?"

Zeke can dish it out but he can't suck it up. "C'mon! Tell me what the buzz is in the newsroom."

"Bing liked it," I said, covering the receiver with my palm. "We did well."

"Shit yeah." Zeke pumped his fist. I also noticed a little pimp in his walk as he began picking up our tapes and stuff.

Angelina had been patient, calmed a bit after the coffee. She said she wanted to lie down in the study. I wasn't going to disturb her until Doug got there.

That boy is the only person I know on the planet who can even come close to driving as fast and as reckless as Zeke. Doug was on that front porch before I knew it.

"Nice job," he said, coming into the house. "Guess you *really* couldn't have called a cop earlier, huh?"

I put my hand on my hip and let my backbone slip. "And let the rest of the world in on what I know?"

"I know how to keep my lips sealed," Doug said, cocking his head back.

"This is true. But like I said before, it's those other liver-lipped folks you work with that I'd be worried about. The ones who get the free tickets from reporters at the other stations."

Doug shrugged. "Jealous?"

"Nope," I said. "Just wanna do my job the best is all. Just like some tall, handsome stop-in-the-name-of-the-law guy I know."

"All right. I'll cut you some slack on this one. So where's this person you want me to talk to, and what's their story?"

"She's Angelina Rosseni, Fab Weaver's cleaning lady. She confirmed the ID of the victim for me and that's how we got in here."

"What makes you think she knows something important?"

"I asked Angelina when was the last time she saw Fab Weaver and she said Saturday afternoon. That's a couple of days before the body was found on Monday. All of a sudden, she gets jumpy. Nervous like. Then she cuts me off."

"Hummpf," Doug said, listening intensely.

"I convinced her to talk to you even though she didn't want to get involved with police. I told Angelina that you would look out for her."

"Good enough. Where is she?"

"In the study."

Doug and I walked in. Angelina was stretched out on the couch, an empty cup of coffee on the end table.

"Angelina?" Doug said softly, touching her shoulder.

She slowly sat up, glanced at Doug, then at me.

"This is Detective Doug Eckart. The officer I was telling you about, Angelina."

She spoke timidly. "Hi."

"Hi." Doug flashed a warm smile. He sat next to her on the couch. "Thanks for cooperating with us. Ms. Barnett tells me that you have something important to tell me. I'm going to ask you some other questions as well. But please don't worry. Just tell me what you know and speak freely, you have nothing to fear."

Angelina immediately relaxed.

"Georgia, I'll handle it from here," Doug said to me.

"Please." Angelina spoke up quickly. "Uhm, can she stay? I—I'd feel better with her in the room. She's been very nice and I'd like her to stay, can she?"

Doug didn't like that. He shrugged reluctantly. "Angelina, that's not how we do things. . . . I promise you this is not going to be an unpleasant experience."

"I know. I guess I'm just a bit shaken up. It's not every day that you hear a man threaten to kill someone, then that person actually turns up dead."

Chapter Six

YOU DROPPED THE BOMB ON ME, BABY!"

Angelina said a mouthful.

"It was over the weekend." Angelina locked her hands together before playing tag with her thumbs. "I was here cooking."

She stopped talking. Breath and apprehension filled her lungs.

"I was in the kitchen, putting water in a pot for mashed potatoes when I looked out into the backyard. It was about one o'clock."

"How do you know what time it was?" Doug asked.

"My favorite cooking show was on cable."

"Okay." Doug made a note to himself. "Go on."

"Umm, Mr. Weaver was standing in the backyard there. He was talking to a man. They started yelling at one another, then the man grabbed Mr. Weaver by the collar with both hands, shook him, then started yelling and screaming."

"What was he saying?" Doug asked.

"He said, 'If you keep fucking with me I'm going to kill you. I mean it. I'll blow your head off!' But he was kind of slurring like he'd been drinking or gotten high."

That son.

"What did Weaver do?" Doug asked.

"He—he knocked the man's hands down, pushed him away. Then Mr. Weaver turned around and came into the house."

Obviously Angelina had come in on the tail end of some mess. Doug began asking her more questions.

"Angelina, did you ask him about what you'd heard and seen?"

"I kindah did. I asked him if he was okay. Mr. Weaver shrugged and mumbled something about he would take care of it."

"What did this other man look like?"

Angelina swallowed like a kid taking a swig of castor oil.

"Ma'am?" Doug prodded.

"He was older, late fifties, African-American . . ."

An *older man and African-American?* Well, it wasn't his son. Doug nudged her on with the next question.

"Was the man dark complexion or light complexion? Tall or short?"

"Dark complexion. Tall, like over six feet. Lanky."

"What was he wearing?"

"A black leather jacket. A turtleneck sweater. A hat, it was over his eyes some. His hair was slicked down in the back."

"Did you see a weapon of any kind?"

"No."

"Do you know what they were arguing about?"

"No."

"Had you seen this man before?"

"He looked familiar. I think he was a musician, one of the guys who used to record for Mr. Weaver. Every now and then he said one of them would come around, begging for money."

"Would you recognize the man again if you saw him?"

"I—I think so."

"I want you to come down to the station . . . work with a sketch artist . . ."

"Not now please, I'm exhausted . . . Couldn't I go home for a while?"

My pager went off. I checked it. It was the assignment desk at Channel 8. The assignment desk is the hub of the newsroom, like the control tower at an airport. Everything crucial has to filter through the assignment desk. They need to know where a reporter is, what's new, how they can help, and logistically where and how the story can get done and into a newscast.

I went out into the hallway and used my cell phone to call in. "Hey, it's me, Georgia, what's up?"

One of the researchers answered the phone and handed it to our boss, Bing. Bing is driven; type-A-plus-plus personality. Loves news and doesn't care how it gets done—just get it first and get it right. Most other news directors let their executive producers and reporters handle their *bizness*; Bing was always out in the newsroom during a big story; always hands-on—on your shoulder or around your neck, that is.

"Nice get, Georgia. What's cooking on the story for the five o'clock news?"

Could I tell him that the police had a vague description of a man who threatened to kill Fab Weaver two days before his body was found? Could I tell him that Angelina may have seen the murderer? No.

Why? Because Doug only let me sit in on the interview after Angelina insisted. I could go with the general but not specifics. Doug would hang me if I tipped off the killer that we had hard clues.

"Bing, they've got a lead but don't want to fork over too many details. They don't have any suspects in custody."

"Bullshit, they know more than that. Georgia, get more info out of those chumps."

"The police aren't in a generous mood today. Don't get me

wrong, Bing. They'll give us something, probably a statement, but not too much more than that. They don't wanna tip off the killer. But who knows, something really huge could break."

"Right. Well, that means you and Zeke will hang around there all day and you might not get anything juicy. We've got this story by the balls, let's keep pulling. . . ."

Please. Some newsroom guys just love to slip into that macho gladiator lingo, like they're really doing something. I'm the one running and gunning, reporting and filming, kicking butt on this story.

"Georgia, we started out with an exclusive. I want us to keep it up; get a nice write-up in the media columns about our coverage."

Can ya smell it? I can. I'm a veteran television reporter. I can smell a wild goose chase coming a mile away, even through Ma Bell's fiberoptic telephone lines, okay? Bing has a tendency to come up with crazy ideas that you have a hell of a time following up on.

"Bing, I should probably hang around here. If nothing develops, then I could do a live shot and rework my earlier material—the shoes, the cleaning lady, the pictures of the victim, his background . . ."

"Hey! Do that. Go dig around more on his background, on that record shit. That's hot stuff, Georgia."

"But then we'll be ass-out here. We need to stay covered. Send someone else and I'll—"

"No. I want you on it. We'll have Clarice and a crew go wait at the house just in case something pops. Meanwhile you can work on giving us a profile of the victim."

"I'd rather stay here in case a relative shows up, talk to the neighbors—"

"You're out of there for now. I want this profile to have some real teeth. Get to digging. Get whatever you can however you can. You already got photos and stuff like that. See if you can find out why someone would want to kill this guy."

I could see Bing pacing up and down as he talked to me. Right about now Bing would sneak a peek at his watch, then issue the challenge. "Georgia, you've got about four hours before the five o'clock news. Show me you've got some balls and dig me up something. Bet ya can. Bye!"

Then my boss hung up the phone.

I could have screamed! I looked back at the study. More about Fab Weaver? I had less than four hours. He was a record producer. The pictures on the wall of the study flashed before my eyes. Fab Weaver in his heyday! Hanging with the boys, the Motown era. Record Row.

Record Row.

That's the logical move for the news groove. I'll just ask Peaches to meet me down there. Sister-twin knows her music history and she's got friends who can help me. I went back into the study, where Doug was talking on the two-way to some of his men who were canvassing the neighborhood.

"Georgia," he said, "one of my men will take Ms. Rosseni home. He'll stay and escort her to the station in a couple of hours. Meanwhile me and some of the boys are gonna go over this study, check out his papers and other records, see what we can turn up. What's your next move?"

"I'm off to do a little profile on Mr. Weaver, got my orders from big chief know-it-all. I would really like to anchor myself here but I can't."

"Well, thank you," Angelina said, "for staying here during my talk with Detective Eckart."

"Anything I can do, just call me," I said and gave her my card with my direct line number at Channel 8.

"Doug, do me a favor. Clarice is coming here to hold down the fort in case something jumps off. Can you ask the guys to keep her in the loop?"

"Done."

Then I was off. Zeke, who was now in the news truck, had his feet up knocked-out asleep. I grabbed Zeke's nose.

"Jesus H. Christ, woman!"

"Drive! Michigan Avenue. Sixteenth Street."

"That's the South Loop. What? You found out where the son is?"

"Naw, we're going to check out Record Row. Or at least what's left of it. We've only got a few hours to piece together a profile on Fab Weaver, one of the wizards of Record Row. And may God forgive me when I say this Zeke, but step on it!"

Zeke yelped for joy, cranked up the truck, and rolled out.

Chapter Seven

RECORD ROW TURNED OUT TO BE KEY.

That same Michigan Avenue far north, known as the Magnificent Mile, where Mr. Martelli's shoe salon was located, had a funkier rep way back in the day. South Michigan Avenue in the fifties, sixties, up until the early seventies, was known as Record Row.

Motown didn't have a *thang* on Record Row.

I knew some of the history. This was the home of record companies, both black- and white-owned. They had the soul sound. Blues. Gospel. Rhythm and blues. Not the smooth pop sound of Motown, the real deal.

I called my sister Peaches, told her to meet at a place she had taken me before called the Game Room. She'd be my passkey. The Game Room is a holdout. A little storefront now surrounded by high-priced condos, lofts, and town houses—price tag $250,000 and up. This little storefront was like a smoke shop. The old-timers would come in and have a cigar, buy some coffee, doughnuts, a burger, play chess and checkers all day. It was like a retirement hangout for old-time musicians.

If they didn't know Record Row no one did.

When Zeke and I got there, Peaches was leaning on her car taking a smoke. She had on a dolphin blue leather jacket, three-quarter length. Dark blue slacks and shoes. Her head was tilted up and angled to the left like she was reading some sheet music floating in the clouds. Peaches flicked her cigarette constantly, even though there were no ashes at the tip. The muscles in her cheeks were contracting. Finally she sensed our presence. Peaches put her cigarette out in the gutter. "Hey, Zeke. What's shaking, sister-twin?"

"Working like a d-o-g. What's wrong with you?"

Peaches shrugged. "Nothing. Tired is all."

Lying like a rug! But I know better than to try and pry it out of her. That would start a throw-down in the middle of the street. *Peaches' temper is rotten, y'all.*

"Well," I said, "perk up. I need your help. I've got to get a story out of these guys. And you've got the gift, girl. Can't nobody make a man open up like you, Peaches."

The truthful compliment was better than a jolt of caffeine. "Come on." Peaches smiled, starting to switch her tail feather. "I wouldn't leave my sister twisting in the wind for neither silver nor gold."

As soon as we walked into the Game Room I knew the person to look for right away. A man named Bang. Bang is the owner. Cool as a hat cocked ace deuce on a pimp's ear, Bang still has presence. He was a drummer in the late sixties and early seventies. Claimed he showed some very famous singers how to put some punch in their songs.

Bang remembered me. Saw me, Zeke, and Peaches walk in and he started drumming on the counter. "*Dig-ah-thing, Dig-ah-thing* . . . look what the wind blew in . . . *dig-ah-thing, dig-ah-thing!*"

"Bang baby!" my sister Peaches howled and gave him a big kiss. She gently patted his back while reintroducing me. "Bang, remember my twin, Georgia?"

"Yes, Lord. Y'all know y'all look about as much alike as a penny and a dime."

The six other men sitting around playing chess, backgammon, and blackjack laughed.

"Well, which do you like better, the penny or the dime?" Peaches batted her eyes.

Sister-twin never misses a chance to flirt.

Bang took Peaches' hand, kissed it, and said, "Baby girl, all money looks good to me!"

"Niggah still talking shit!" one of the guys yelped out.

"I like it in him!" another complimented.

"Who's the hard leg?" one of the old musicians asked, pointing a thumb at Zeke after he moved a red checker across the board.

"Name's Zeke," my cameraman said.

"He's going to help me catch you guys on videotape talking about Record Row."

"At last—at last!" A chess man primped. "Point that camera *right here*, baby. Shoot my good side."

"You sitting on it," his buddy joked across the board.

I pulled up a chair. Zeke set up the shot. I set the tone. "I want you guys to talk a little bit about Record Row. What it was like. Then talk about anything and all you know about Fab Weaver."

"Oh that motherfucker!" someone shouted.

"No sympathy here!" someone else growled. "Best use of a grave I've ever heard of."

I was a bit stunned by their sheer animosity. These men did not hold back. They were fierce. They nearly spat on the floor at the mere mention of Fab Weaver's name. "Was Fab Weaver that bad? Who would want to kill him?"

"You mean outside of every musician in this room?"

"What?"

"Listen, Fab Weaver and his company, Hit Time Records, was the biggest rip-off on Record Row," one of the men playing checkers explained. "He made millions. Had checks crossing his desk that had more zeros than a can of SpaghettiOs. And didn't pay the cats making the music squat!"

"We didn't make no money," another musician said, tapping a cane in his hand then pointing to a picture on the wall. "But we looked good. That's me there with the bass, flush right and fine."

"We were jamming," Bang said, laughing and drumming out a new beat on the bar. "Gold record after gold record and that ain't no lie, baby sister."

"Just stayed broke," another musician interjected. "Broke as the day is long."

"One white producer bought me a Caddy!" a backgammon player said whimsically. "Didn't know he owned the dealership. Thought it was mine, but when I wouldn't give a song I wrote for myself to a new group he was trying to push, repo man showed up and yanked it away. That kind of bullshit happened all the time."

"Let me be devil's advocate here," I said. "Most of the record companies shorted royalties. That's pretty much common knowledge. But was it really as bad as you say?"

Everyone began grumping and groaning at once, throwing up their hands like sinners shouting at a tent revival hosted by the devil.

"Hey, guys," I said trying to get some order and struggling to hide my excitement. This interview was going to be hot—and it was going to be real. "We can't edit the piece if everybody talks at once. One at a time, okay?"

"All right fellahs," Bang said, calming his friends down, "let me start it off on the A side of this tune. Record Row was fabulous. Motown was famous because it whitewashed R&B, prettied it up for the mainstream. But all Detroit had was Motown. On Record Row there was Vee-Jay, Brunswick, Chess, Fab Weaver's Hit Time Records, and more. . . ."

"Etta James was at Chess," the old bass player said raising his cane. "She gave a gospel flavor to the new soul sound *before* Aretha Franklin!"

Peaches chimed in off camera, "Curtis Mayfield. Fontella Bass. The Dells. And . . . uh . . ."

"The Beatles!" Bang said. "They loved soul music. Some of their early recordings were released on Vee-Jay right here in Chicago. They left in a fight over money, signed with Capitol records. Then they exploded—blam!!!"

"Did Fab Weaver have any influence on WVON and what songs were played?"

"Little girl, what you know about that!" Bang teased me before slapping a sideways five with one of his boys.

I know some history too now! "Chicago had the first twenty-four-hour all-black radio station—WVON. Stands for Voice of the Negro! They played the hits and reported all the latest civil rights news too."

"You go, girl!" Bang said, eyes sparkling. "Don Cornelius was a DJ at WVON. Soul Train started right here in Chicago!"

"Right. But the sad part," one of the musicians continued, "was that we didn't make any money. Fab Weaver was the worst of the bunch. If the average white record producer made a hundred thousand off your record, he might give you five grand. Fab Weaver? He'd give you one grand and keep you in a clothing account."

"That's on a good day!" one of the checker players hurmped. "Every song somebody wrote, Fab Weaver put his name on it. Kept all the rights to the songs and most of the royalty money too. Liked his talent young—teenagers, so he could bully 'em easier, keep 'em in check."

The cane thumped hard twice on the floor. "Listen here. That old slick Weaver used to bring kids up from the South. Green as pole beans. No book learning but talented. Give 'em a steak. Dress 'em up. Put 'em on the stage at the Regal Theatre, then steal all their songs."

"If Fab Weaver could read music!" one musician shouted, "I can read Braille! He was a stone crook."

Another musician added, "And he really took those guys, The Locomotions. They had two gold records in '68 and wasn't none of them over eighteen years old."

"Yep," one of the musicians said, leaning back in his chair, stroking his chin. "I remember when those cats hit town. Wanted to call themselves The Teenagers, but you know that was the name of Frankie Lymon's backup."

The bass player began twisting the cane between his palms. "Fab Weaver called them The Locomotions 'cause they had gotten thrown off three different trains before they finally made it to Chicago. Say, Bang, you and Jimmy used to play sessions for them, huh?"

"Just a couple of times. We wasn't nothing but eighteen ourselves," Bang replied easily. "All those cats are gone now."

The cane thumped against the floor again. "Worried themselves sick over being beat out of their money all these years."

"So you see, young lady," another musician explained, "ain't no pity party here for Fab Weaver or none of those other record executives who lived like kings off our songs."

"Damn right," one of the guys said, flipping a red checker in the air like a coin. "I sold over a million records in my day and can't afford health insurance. Can't afford to help my grandson through college."

"None of us," the bass player panned around the room with his cane, "have retirement plans. No royalty money when one of these young cats decides to hip-hop our music."

"Hell, Fab Weaver is lucky he lived as long as he did!" another musician noted. "He probably just cheated the wrong person and it caught up with him."

"Yeah. Flamingo was in here last week, said he'd blow the man away next time he laid eyes on him . . ." Bang said, his voice trailing.

Flamingo? I thought. "Jimmy?" I asked.

"Yeah, but oh," Bang chuckled, "Jimmy didn't really mean it, naw. . . ."

Angelina's description of the suspect. Older African-American . . .

". . . he was mad is all. We were sitting here watching TV when one of those new car commercials came on . . ."

. . . Dark complexion. Tall like over six feet. Lanky.

". . . the music they were using was one of Jimmy Flamingo's songs. Fab Weaver stole the rights to it. That's when Jimmy said he wanted to blow him away."

"Aww, Bang, you always making something out of nothing," one of the men said easily. "That wasn't nothing at all. Jimmy was just talking."

"I know that man," Bang whined, "Jimmy Flamingo is my friend. I knew him way before you."

Angelina's description of the man who threatened to kill Fab Weaver loomed in my mind. I turned to my sister.

"Peaches, did Jimmy ever say anything about Fab Weaver to you?"

Peaches shrugged, then shook her head no.

"Well, he never called Fab Weaver by his full name like that," Bang explained to me.

"What would he call him?" I asked.

"Hit Time. Just like the record company. That's because he *was* the record company. He called every shot."

Suddenly my twin sister looked like she needed oxygen.

"Peaches, are you okay?"

"Gimme a minute," Peaches said. "At the car."

"Hey, Georgia"—Bang touched my shoulder—"listen, sweetheart, let's take a stroll down the street. I'mah show you where all the record companies were located. Start with Chess on Fourteenth Street. Do even better. I'll even let you take a couple of old pictures I've got on the walls out back as long as you return them."

"Zeke, can you go with Bang down the block? Let him walk and talk the video pointing out key locations. Shoot it tight, like he's talking directly to the audience. I'll catch up."

Outside, Peaches had her head down, leaning on the hood, examining her feet. "Georgia, Jimmy's been acting funny."

My shoulders slumped. You know how you can just feel it when some mess is about to start? That's how I felt.

"Jimmy called me. He was very upset, just like he'd been a few nights before. He was high, slurring. Yelling. I screamed back at him. Then Jimmy said he wasn't going to show up this weekend at the club and hung up on me."

"Where is he now, Peaches?"

"No tellin', sister-twin. When you called my cell phone I had just left his apartment after not getting an answer. I don't have time to find another act, shit. Now, I'm really worried though. I'm trying to get this thing together in my mind."

"What's up?"

"This ain't easy to figure out, Georgia. See, I wasn't that worried at first cause Jimmy, you know, he starts to drink sometimes to keep from doing the drugs. Goes on a binge for a day or so but then he gets over that—"

"Skip that. What's eating at you, Peaches?"

"Jimmy gets nasty when he drinks, very nasty, and most of the time, he can't remember a thing afterwards. Says it must be the whiskey slow-dancing with the coke he did at one time. Rocks him to sleep. He goes off, then, to sleep."

"And you're telling me all this because?"

"Will you just listen, Georgia? Jimmy was throwing a fit and he said something about how the music business was killing him, how he hated Hit Time and wanted to see him in his grave. Now, with what Bang said and the man dead, kindah shook a twin up, ya know what I'm saying?"

"Girl," I told Peaches, "we need to go to the police and tell them what you know. The news hasn't broke yet, but there's a cleaning lady who saw a man threatened to kill Fab Weaver at his home."

"So?" Peaches shrugged.

"So, Miss Thing, the description is sketchy but it sounds an awful lot like Jimmy."

Peaches cussed under her breath. "It's got to be just a coincidence."

"What?"

Peaches shrugged again. I knew there was something more she wasn't telling me.

"What, Peaches?"

"Well, Jimmy had a gun too. But it's nothing—"

"Nothing, my behind. You said gun, Peaches. You mean Jimmy might've been shooting off more than his mouth?"

"Georgia, damn. He wasn't wearing it on his hip like the Lone Ranger. He had it in a drawer. I saw it when I was picking him up for band rehearsal a couple of weeks ago. See, I'm jumpy and you're making me jumpier. Let's just find Jimmy—"

"Let me call Doug."

"A cop? Please!"

"It's Doug, Peaches."

"A cop by any other name is still *The Man.*"

"Oh, what's that supposed to mean?"

"I like Doug. I like you with him, sister-twin. But we've only known Doug a few months. And he's a lawman. He's going to put the law first. If you think this kindah looks suspect to you, how do you think it'll look to a detective? The cops will throw Jimmy in the lockup now and ask questions later. That'll sure as hell throw Jimmy off the wagon quick."

"So what do you want to do?"

"I know a couple of places Jimmy might be, I want you to go with me and have my back!"

"Peaches—Doug won't—"

"See, that's what I'm talking about, Georgia. I ask you to back a twin up, end of story. And what do you do? Hem and haw."

"Don't try to play me, Peaches. This could be dangerous. This looks funky and you *know* it."

"But Jimmy is a good guy. I can't believe he's a cold-blooded killer. I've got to talk to him."

"People shock you all the time. If nothing else I've learned that from working in TV news doing story after story."

"Look, I believe in Jimmy. Back me up or get the hell out of my way," Peaches said going to the driver's side, getting in.

Dontcha just hate it? Family can make you do stuff you don't wanna do. All day and tomorrow too.

I opened the passenger side of the car and stuck my head in. "Just chill, Hot Mama. Let me call into the station and tell them I'm sick. My story's basically written. I'll get Zeke to record it in the truck. There's a recording device and a microphone; only takes about twenty minutes to do. So cool your jets, Peaches. I'll have to get Zeke to take that and all the other interviews and b-roll back to the station; a writer can put it together easily." I sighed. "Then we'll get busy. I've got your back, in all ways. And don't you ever again fix those big liver lips of yours to question that."

Then I slammed the door. I wish I owned a crystal ball, a viewfinder into the future, or could read tarot cards. But all I had was the veil I was born with, the thin layer of skin over the eyes, easily removed but ultimately revealing an extraordinary gift of instinct. The hair on the back of my neck was twitching. Had an *ugly-wugly* feeling. But who knew that in less than twenty-four hours both Peaches and me would land in a hospital emergency room?

Chapter Eight

JIMMY FLAMINGO IS A G-MAN: A GUITAR MAN, A GET-HIGH man, and a gambling man.

Peaches took us straight to an abandoned brick three-flat on Forty-fifth and Stewart. We walked around the rear, and right near the corner was a door with a buzzer and an intercom. Now mind you the place was all boarded up except for this door, and the intercom was out-of-the-box new. The voice pouring from it was a whiskey baritone. "Password?"

"Leadbelly," Peaches said.

"C'mon down."

"Down?" I questioned.

Don't you know Peaches just kept on walking? She walked very dainty-like too, as if we were on a red carpet instead of crumbled concrete and broken glass. And when we got buzzed in? It was deep. *Literally!* We must have walked about three feet forward to a set of steps; from there it was straight down. It was steep and black. Like some kind of a coal mine.

"Girl, you always did like the low end. When Mama would dress us up on Sunday and take us to visit one of our little church friends, no sooner than she'd leave, you'd sneak out the back way and make a beeline for the projects."

"Those project kids were fun! And they were the same as us, just with less money. And it ain't like we were rich. We struggled. But our mama is what you call uppity. I'm what you call real."

"And what am I?"

"Georgia, you're whatcha call 'tween. You'll go on the low end, but you won't stay long."

Peaches' hearty laughter was swallowed up by a macho, reckless, exciting sound. My ears were completely done in by the noise, my eyes nearly blinded by the smoke and the searing yellow haze thrown off by a naked 120-watt bulb.

In the center of a huge cellar was a makeshift floor, hardwood planks cut six feet long laid side by side. About eight guys were hunched over shooting craps. The game was running high; they ignored the two folding chairs near a tabletop with brown-tinted bottles and clear shot glasses. And these men, baby, I mean they were clean! Not a pair of jeans or work slacks among 'em. Suits. What South Siders call Mades. That's short for tailor-made, flamboyant colors with unique cut collars and cuffs. Patent leather shoes and hats with brims so wide they had to call into the control tower at O'Hare Airport to reserve airspace.

"Doggone," I whispered.

"Yeah," Peaches said, leaning into my ear. "This is the low end but there's big money here. Look at that pile."

Cash, baby, cash! New bills. Old bills. Just bills. Big ones. All draped over one another, displayed and desirable; the white dice bumped, rolled, and teased over the fifty- and one-hundred-dollar notes.

Peaches grabbed me. "Look at Jimmy!"

Jimmy was hunched over, legs cocked open like a frog's, the veins of his black silk socks crooked. His suit, not as expensive as the others, not quite as well fitting as the others, showed that on most days he was the least favored of these lucky men. But Jimmy had his brim cocked back, nearly falling off the rear of his skull, wearing a big smile, his right hand stuffed with money, his left cradling the dice. On this day, all the luck in the world was in his wrist. "Here we go . . . Yah. Hit it."

The crowd yelled, "Awwww!"

Jimmy grabbed the money. "Hot damn!"

"Now," Peaches whispered, "does that look like a killer to you?"

"Hey, Peaches, Georgia!" Jimmy said, standing up, the spaces between his fingers fat with greenbacks. "I'm hot as hell."

"And in deep trouble!" Peaches scolded. "You can't just cancel your club date, Jimmy. What's the matter with you anyway?"

"Easy, woman," Jimmy said, coming over to us. "I apologize about wolfing at you, Peaches. I couldn't help it. All my debts were coming down on me, and I mean hard. But my luck done broke. I can't lose. I'm cleaning my partners out. Here, this is for you, baby sister."

Jimmy took a one-hundred-dollar bill and held it out to Peaches. "Get yourself something nice."

"But you're trying to get back on your feet."

Jimmy wrapped his arms around our shoulders and turned us into an intimate circle. "Let you in on a secret. I've got enough money to catch up on my rent, my car note, and then some."

"In that case . . ." Peaches snatched the bill out of his hand and stuffed it down her bra. "That money goes in the vault, baby."

"Trifling!" I cut my eyes at Peaches. Then I made sure she was looking dead in my face when I said, "Ask him."

"Whaaaattt . . ." Peaches whined, dropping her eyes.

"Ask me what?"

"Jimmy!" one of the men yelled. "Get back over here. You got all the money."

"Hold up, man!" Jimmy said over his shoulder. "Hold up!"

Peaches plays tough girl, but she'll wimp out in a minute when she has to get tough with somebody she cares about. Like her three-year-old son Satch, one of her men, or someone she idolizes. Somebody like Jimmy. But not me and Mama. She gives us the vapors—a hot fit when your blood pressure rises during a heated argument. I had to rap to Jimmy myself.

"Jimmy," I said softly, "let's go outside and talk. It's serious."

"Something serious? Oh, is that why y'all are here? Something serious."

"No, we're here for our health," I said sarcastically.

"Damn, Jimmy, man! Bring your black ass on. Stop acting like a punk letting a couple of bitches hold up the game. . . ."

Jimmy spun around, lurched forward, and dropped the nasty-mouthed one with a short punch to the gut. He was a younger man than the rest of the crowd; late thirties, tried to have the look of these seasoned players but one good glance and you could tell right off the bat that brother man was missing it—and never would have it.

"Ricky," Jimmy said, looking down at him. "Don't disrespect me or any woman hanging with me."

A steamy evil flooded Ricky's eyes as he rubbed his gut with his hand. "Well, you got all the money. Plenty of it's mine. What's the big deal? I just meant hurry up, damn."

Jimmy extended his hand to the young man and pulled him up. "And that's why you still ain't a player. You don't rush a winner, baby. Look'ah here. Take this twenty. I don't want you to go home busted."

"I'm not going nowhere!"

"Oh, you off the scene, young blood," Jimmy said. "G'on. C'mon back to play another day when your luck and your attitude is better."

Some of the old players chuckled.

Ricky ignored the money and left.

"Jimmy," one of the gamblers said, "I wouldn't have gone through all that nonsense. I'd shot that young buck in his ass disrespecting me like that. Where's your piece, man?"

"Gone." He shrugged. "Somebody stole it. Now, back to the game."

"Jimmy," I grabbed his arm. "Fab Weaver is dead. . . ."

"I know and ain't shame to say that I shouted for joy when I heard the news. He's history!"

"Yeah," I said, "but what I want to know is did you help history?"

"What?" Jimmy looked at Peaches.

"Georgia thinks, well, you hated the man."

"So she thinks I murdered him?" Jimmy's laugh was warm but penetrating. "And you worry about me using drugs. Georgia, you must be on crack if you think I'm a killer."

"Save the jokes for 'Comic View,'" I said. "I'm just saying that you're someone the police will want to talk to. A cleaning lady heard a man fitting your description threaten to shoot Fab Weaver during an argument at his house."

"That was me! Saturday? I went over to talk to that chump about the money he owed me. Sure I told him I'd kill him. It was just talk, woman. Couldn't help it, I was mad. But listen here, I ain't crazy. I didn't shoot nobody, Georgia."

"But Jimmy, he was killed with a twenty-two just like you like to carry."

"I don't care if he was killed with a bow and arrow and I was Robin Hood. I ain't kill nobody!"

Jimmy yelled that last part. The dice stopped rolling then. Everyone was eyeballing us in the corner.

"Jimmy. Peaches. Let's just go out to the car where we can talk freely."

"Why?" He cussed under his breath. "Why break my luck?"

"All I'm saying is this, let's go to the police before they come looking for you. Peaches and I will go with you. Let me call Doug."

"To hell with Doug. You oughtah know better, Georgia."

"That's what I told her!" Peaches said, jumping on his side.

I got mad at my twin. "Peaches, you know good and doggone well that things are looking fishy. Otherwise you wouldn't have brought me here."

Jimmy's gaze sliced Peaches.

"I'm here because I care about Jimmy. Period."

Jimmy's gaze softened. "Let's go outside so I can clear this up with y'all right now."

We headed back up the dark and dingy tunnel through which we had come. Outside was heavenly. The air was cold and crisp inside my lungs. The clouds looked like stacks of dishes soaking in the sudsy blue sky.

"How can you guys stay in that hole down there and gamble like that?" I wondered out loud.

"We've got whiskey. We've got a toilet. What else do we need?" Jimmy answered as we walked toward Peaches' car. "Vegas ain't the only place where big money can be won!"

"Or lost," a voice behind us said. "Don't move!"

We turned around slowly.

"Come off that load," Ricky ordered Jimmy. He was in a crouch with a blade. It was slim, long, and silver, and looked like a natural extension of his hand, as if he'd actually grown a devil's claw. Ricky's scowl was merciless and straight from hell.

Jimmy smiled. "Don't you know I hate knives, man?"

"And I hate to lose." Ricky swiped with the knife. Jimmy jumped back and Peaches and I clutched each other. "Give it up, big mouth. And go slow, old man, go slow."

Jimmy began reaching in his pocket. The block was deserted. No cars except the ones belonging to the players who were still inside hustling the game. Vacant lots and abandoned buildings were our only witnesses.

Jimmy pulled out a wad of bills, damp from the mildewed base-ment and the sweaty palms that had reluctantly given them up. He held his hand out and the bills dropped in a clump like a used tea bag.

Ricky's eyes followed the money.

Jimmy pushed Peaches and me back with one hand and whipped his jacket off with the other. "Come on, young buck. You wanna make your bones off old Jimmy, c'mon then."

The blade lurched toward Jimmy's right side and like a bull-fighter he smoothly slipped it. Left lunge. The same suave slip. Jimmy sidestepped and swung. He missed and Ricky slashed low, catching Jimmy on the leg. "Aww, God!"

Ricky slashed high. Jimmy flinched and the blade's tip grazed his forehead.

"Let him have the money, Jimmy!" I shouted. Ricky leaned forward shoving the knife in my face, then backed off to face Jimmy again.

Jimmy sneered and began whipping his jacket like he was trying to put out a fire. Ricky backpedaled. Jimmy rushed him. Ricky lost his balance, lowering the arm that held the knife. Jimmy managed to catch the pesky blade in the meat of his jacket.

Ricky stared at Jimmy with fear. Jimmy punched him in the face. Ricky went down on one knee and then caught Jimmy around the calf with his free hand and yanked him down. Peaches screamed her lungs out! Ricky slammed Jimmy's head against the curb, rolled away, grabbed the money, and began tearing up the street.

Two streams of crimson ran on separate paths along Jimmy's body—from his leg and his head, forming a thin crest bordered by his bent elbow and clenched fist. "Damn!"

By now the gambling men had come. The cavalry they ain't. They watched as Ricky hopped a sagging, chain-link fence. "I ain't chasing that young cat!" one of the men said. "Got something for him though, if I ever lay eyes on him again."

"Call an ambulance," I said.

One of the guys whipped out his cell phone. Another one asked, "You ladies all right?"

Peaches nodded, her body shaking as she leaned against the car. I was too busy to answer, examining Jimmy's forehead. Flesh wound, not bad. His leg. *Whose bad.* Major stitches.

The gamblers grumped and grumbled about their losses, the lack of respect for seasoned players like them, what they were gonna do to that punk Ricky whenever they got their hands on him.

Jimmy held his ground, clenching his teeth, "Sssszzzz!"

"Hang on," Peaches said. "I hear the siren. Finally. It's coming."

Chapter Nine

ISN'T IT A LOW-DOWN DIRTY SHAME HOW MANY DIFFERENT ways we can hurt one another? The emergency room of the county hospital was packed.

One man in the corner of the room was sitting with his arm wrapped in a bloody towel, the tip of what looked like a fork sticking out.

One woman sat across the room with her face viciously scratched, a track of skin missing from her cheek.

A teenage boy was on a gurney, waiting to go into the next examining room beyond the white curtain that shielded the waiting and concerned from the injured. Both the teenager's arms had been broken in a gang fight.

Jimmy had beaten the evening crime rush in the big city. It wasn't even six o'clock yet and the emergency room was jumping. Pity for the city that unseasonable warmth sometimes means acting a fool to people who get outside and just don't know what to do with themselves. All these trauma cases arrived after we did.

Peaches sat in the corner moping, still very much shaken up by the armed robbery and shooting. I wasn't in the best of moods either. It wasn't every day that I was in the middle of drama that involved me in such a personal way.

I went to the pop machine. I slipped in some quarters and chose a Diet Coke. I swigged it down, the liquid firecracker exploding inside my mouth. My body craved the caffeine but really desired rest more than anything. I tried to call in to the station on the sly and get Clarice but the hospital waiting area was not allowing me a clear signal on my cell. I walked back into the emergency room and stopped trying when I realized that there was a television set in the corner.

It was almost time for the five o'clock news. I asked one of the staffing nurses if I could turn on the television. She recognized me immediately, gushed, and said certainly. She asked if everything was okay. I said wishfully, "Gonna be." I told her I was accompanying my sister, who was here with a hurt friend.

I used the remote to flick to Channel 8 before jacking up the sound. Bass and driving cymbals rang out; this royal music processional always ushered in our evening newscast.

The top story of the day? It happened to be a factory fire in suburban Westmont. Channel 8's chopper hovered over the blaze; the payoff shots were the smoke and ruby-trimmed flames shooting up from the collapsing rooftop. People in nearby homes were being forced to evacuate.

The other top story in the show was mine. I listened as our anchorman, Dan, read the intro:

"In other news tonight . . . we now know more about the murdered man whose body was discovered along Manning Pier. Earlier this afternoon, in a Channel 8 exclusive, we were the first to identify the victim as Fab Weaver, a retired record executive."

The director put up a full-screen graphic, a picture of Fab Weaver mounted on a blue background with his last name in bold white letters. Dan read on:

"Tonight we give you a glimpse into the life of the man who once ran one of the most powerful and ruthless companies on Chicago's famed Record Row.

"WJIV's Georgia Barnett has all the details."

Dan looked down at his desk monitor and the director took my package, which was recorded on tape. It opened up with the natural sound of Bang's voice under an old picture of Hit Time Records on Sixteenth and Michigan back in 1968.

"Hit Time Records," Bang began to explain. The shot pushed slowly into the photo. "It had the best sound studio in town but it was run by Fab Weaver. He was the most cutthroat man on Record Row."

There was a dissolve from the photo to Bang standing outside the same spot today looking wistfully at the building, which was now being turned into a condo. My voice track came in under the picture.

"Meet Bang Robinson. He's a gatekeeper. He keeps alive the memories and the history of Record Row, once a thriving business located here on South Michigan Avenue. He, along with many other musicians, worked for the murder victim, Fab Weaver. Weaver, shown here in a 1968 photo with the group The Locomotions, is accused of using strong-arm tactics to force musicians to sign over the rights to their songs. The songs were a gold mine then, and they're a gold mine now."

Stop my track and up comes the natural sound of a new car commercial.

"We're on the fast lane to love . . ."

The hip sixties R&B sound hummed as the sports car sped along a hilly mountain road. My narration picked up again.

"The credit line of the song used in this commercial says written and produced by Fab Weaver."

Cut to b-roll shots of Weaver's den with all the gold records.

"It says the same thing on these gold records adorning his wall. But is this fact or is it fiction?"

Cut to a wide setup shot of the musicians at the Game Room.

"The answer is fiction, according to this core group of Chicago musicians. They say it's all an ugly facade. That Fab Weaver never wrote, produced, or performed—he simply stole."

Stop my voice track and fade up back-to-back sound bites from the musicians talking about Fab Weaver.

"If Fab Weaver could read music, I can read Braille!"

"Weaver used to bring kids up from the South. Green as pole beans. No book learning but talented. Give 'em a steak. Dress 'em up. Put 'em on the stage at the Regal Theatre, then steal all their songs."

"Hell, Fab Weaver is lucky he lived as long as he did! He probably just cheated the wrong person and it caught up with him."

Cut to file shots from Monday afternoon, Fab Weaver's body in a black bag being loaded into a paddy wagon at Manning Pier.

"Caught up with him means this, shot in the back and dumped in Lake Michigan. Acquaintances of Fab Weaver say he is survived by an adult son named Guy. So far police have not been able to locate him, so the body of this retired millionaire record producer remains in the county morgue and his killer remains at large. Georgia Barnett, WJIV News."

Dump tape to take Dan for a live on-camera tag.

"Some of the well-known recordings to be produced on Record Row are 'Rescue Me,' 'Something's Got a Hold on Me,' and 'People Get Ready.' Brunswick Records was the last to close its doors on Record Row, doing so in the mid-1970s."

I was happy with my piece. The writer did a nice job putting it together in my absence back at the station. I turned around and Jimmy was walking toward us, his head adorned in a bandage as fine as eyelet lace. One pants leg was cut off high on the thigh revealing a thick white bandage. Jimmy walked gingerly on his injured leg.

Peaches teased him. "Well, you look a mess!"

"I feel a mess! An aching head and five stitches in my leg. I've had better days."

A doctor was with him, dressed in green scrubs, splattered with sprinkles of dried blood. He was a young doctor, African-American, small build, a beard, sensitive eyes that steadied themselves on me. "The leg wound was more bloody than anything else. He'll have a scar to brag about but nothing more. But that head injury is another thing. The flesh wound isn't bad but he took a couple of punches to the head too."

"Well, do you need to keep him?" Peaches said, her mouth snapping back shut, tense with worry.

"No!" Jimmy said like a judge closing a case. "I wanna get out of here, now."

The doctor ignored Jimmy and continued to speak to Peaches and me. "Is there someone who can stay with him, to keep an eye on him? Head wounds can be tricky. If he develops headaches, gets dizzy, or becomes nauseous, someone will need to bring him in right away."

Before either Peaches or I could answer, someone else volunteered for the job, but baby, it was not a good thing.

"We'll keep an eye on him, Doc," a voice behind us volunteered. "And you know what? We'll have a little talk with our friend Jimmy too."

We all turned around and there were Doug and a white detective. It had been the white detective who spoke, his words towering, like his height, a full head over Doug, who was no little man. The detective's piercing blue eyes demanded attention; his body, thick as a slab of concrete, demanded obeying.

Doug stood next to him, assured, his face forthright yet purely unhappy. He was clearly the backup man for this encounter.

"Jimmy Flamingo," the detective said, "you're coming with us

down to the station. We want to talk to you about the murder of Fab
Weaver."

The detective quickly patted Jimmy down. This was going to be
ugly. I could feel it in my bones, drama in the game. I was being
pulled into it; had my people with me though to help. Peaches was in
it. Jimmy was in it. Doug was in it.

The white detective grabbed Jimmy by the arm, "C'mon. We just
wanna talk."

Jimmy's body recoiled. "I didn't do nothing!"

Doug stepped forward now, his suit jacket hanging heavy across
his broad shoulders, yet not as heavy as the look in his eyes when
they met mine. He took Jimmy by the arm, and said sympathetically,
"Jimmy, I'll walk with you."

Peaches sneered. "That's awful big of you."

Jimmy?

His face went cold, the way a weather front off the lake chills a
Chicago night. Cold that cuts through your clothes quick and fine
like a street switchblade. Jimmy's eyes emptied themselves of emotion and hardened into plates of steel, shielding him from the
knowing stares of strangers in the emergency room.

Jimmy was used to rocking the world; now his world was being
rocked.

He looked up once at Peaches, then at me. Breath was the only
force still offering resistance, still showing some rustle of life. It was
Jimmy's breath that pleaded his case, simply. "I ain't done nothing."

All I could think of was, do I believe him? Belief is a principle
that digs at the soul, pulling at the unreasonable, picking at the
impossible, jousting with the unlikely. I reasoned with the issues
and the nagging questions.

Jimmy's hate of the man he called Hit Time was pure and anything pure can shock the system, causing it to erupt. Had his hate erupted into murder? That required me to think if Jimmy was likely to be not just capable of murder. Being a veteran reporter has sho' nuff shown me that anyone is capable of anything. But was Jimmy likely?

Jimmy was shaking his head now, talking to Doug, "Man, what?"

Doug didn't say anything to soothe him, but handled him gently, walked him slow, saved him the embarrassment of cuffs. Doug looked over his shoulder and mouthed to me the word "Lawyer."

Then Jimmy jerked around, growling with a pitiful flavor, "As soon as you came around me all this shit started. Go home, Peaches!"

"But Jimmy—"

"Go home. You're bad luck, Peaches, damn, go on!"

Peaches stood there watching, turned into stone by the power of Jimmy's rebuke. When they left, two seconds after they were gone, Peaches began to chip. First her eyes watered. Then she wrung her hands until a strip of white ash whisked itself across her knuckles. Then Peaches wondered, "How did they know Jimmy was here?"

Then those chips of anger turned to stone and sister-twin began to hurl them at me. "How'd the police know we were here, huh?"

"I don't know, Peaches." *How did they know?*

Peaches started rocking. Don't she realize I know that doggone rock? Probably felt it in the womb as we lay crisscross. Saw it every time she got mad at Bucket, the little boy next door who loved to grab her candy bag and run. Peaches would get mad and stay mad, repeat the same question like a needle skipping back to the same beat on a scratched forty-five.

Peaches kept rocking, then glanced up and sighed. She had a thought. "I mean damn, how'd they know? In particular, Doug."

"I wish I knew all the sources Doug has, informants here and there; a keen instinct too."

"And a squeeze who is a reporter!"

She thinks I dropped a dime on Jimmy? "You think I told him? How? I can't even get a signal in here on my cell phone. Or was it mental telepathy? I've been with you every minute."

"Until you went to get a pop. And I can see with my own two eye-balls that there's a pay phone right next to the pop machine!"

Now see, Peaches wanted to be beat down. After I have left work under false pretenses to help her. Gone into that grungy gambling pit and had a knife stuck in my face. Sat up in the county hospital emergency room holding her damn hand. Now I'm a snitch; it doesn't pay to be Flo Nightingale with some folks, period.

"After all this drama today! You've got the nerve to stand there and accuse me of backstabbing you and Jimmy. Have you lost your mind? Girl, please!"

"That's all that makes sense, Georgia. You wanted to call Doug all along."

"And?"

"So you just went ahead and called him, thinking you were help-ing, but really you were screwing everything up. Jimmy's mad with me because of you."

That made me angry. "Peaches, there's good news and bad news. The good news is we're in a hospital emergency room. The bad news is you're about to need a bed!"

The one thing that stopped me from wringing her fool neck was my pager firing up. I looked. I rolled my eyes. "Work!"

Peaches was mad but not stupid. She knew it was time for us to get out of each other's way. "I'm going to call Jimmy's niece. She used to be a paralegal. I bet she knows some good lawyers. Maybe his family won't sell him out!"

Then she bolted.

Hit and run.

I went to the pay phone that Peaches had falsely accused me of using. This time I called in to the assignment desk. Clarice answered the phone. "Georgia, it's funky *up in here, up in here!*"

She was whispering. Something had jumped off. My heart took on an unsteady beat—slow, then fast. I waited for Clarice to clarify.

"Bing is in Scud Missile mode."

"Why? My piece was good. I gave him what he asked for."

"But," Clarice continued to whisper, "Channel 5 had the attorney."

"What attorney?"

"Fab Weaver's attorney. They interviewed him. He said that the blues singer—Jimmy Flamingo? him—that he had threatened Fab Weaver in the past and they had an order of protection against him."

Doggone it! The competition gave up Jimmy as the prime suspect and in the process they scooped me. "Ugh! Bing wants to hang me up by the thumbs now and cane me, huh?"

"Georgia, you know you're my homegirl, right?"

Awww, this was bad if she was playing me like this.

"But I would not want to be nowhere near you right now. That's what I hate about news. When things are bad, they are horrid, know what I'm saying?"

"Yeah, yeah, just hit me with it already." I braced myself.

"Everybody knows you didn't go home sick either. . . ."

"How?"

"Because we just got a phone tip from one of the nurses there. She called in and said that Jimmy Flamingo got hauled off to jail after being treated for a knife wound. She said you and your sister were there helping him. Wanted to know if we'd pay her for the news tip."

"If it wasn't for buzzard luck, Clarice, I wouldn't have no luck at all."

"Well, they sent Brent Manning to the cop shop to wait for them to walk Jimmy Flamingo. . . ."

I didn't want to hear anymore. I didn't need to hear anymore.

Jimmy was mad at Peaches. Peaches was mad at me. I was mad at Doug. I was in dutch at my TV gig. Could it get any worse? That's what I'm saying. How could I fix it?

Chapter Ten

I COULD FIX IT BY GOING TO SEE THE LAWYER, FAB WEAVER'S lawyer who had been exclusively interviewed by Channel 5. I got scooped. Hey, it happens. Sometimes you get the bear and sometimes the bear gets you. But I couldn't help thinking that if I had not been messing around with Peaches I wouldn't have erred in my coverage. I really didn't regret it; had to back up my knuckle-headed sister even though she acted like she didn't appreciate it one bit.

Peaches can get like that when she becomes upset; whatever the issue is becomes her universe and she wallows in it. I don't wallow. I swim. Now I'm about to make an Olympic level move on this story by getting to Fab Weaver's lawyer. Channel 5 did not, and smartly so, say where the attorney worked. That was their way of saying, *Nah-nah, we got him and you can't find him!*

TV news can get kiddy like that sometimes.

But Angelina told me that her checks came directly from Weaver's lawyer. She couldn't remember his name but would look at her pay stub when she got home.

Did Angelina remember?

I prayed she had. My energy was starting to wane and an old-fashioned bloodhound search for this lawyer would take too much of my precious time.

I called my answering machine at home. I had a message from my mother, who was mad as a queen bee because I hadn't been by and hadn't called. Mama didn't play that. She was tripping too. But I was wrong; have to mend that later.

I called my voice mail at work, punched in my code. No message from Angelina. Then I called Clarice, my backup on the assignment desk.

"I've got to redeem myself. I need to get to Fab Weaver's attorney. Did you see the coverage on Channel 5?"

"Yep," Clarice said, "and I know you can't stand getting beat. As soon as I saw him pop up on the screen I wrote his name down and got to work."

"My girl," I said relieved. "Clarice, did I ever tell you that you're tremendous? Outstanding? Supreme?"

"But more important, I'm fine!"

Clarice is real and I love her for it.

"The attorney's name is Horace Hightower. There's a Hightower and Loeb located on Lasalle. I called there, told the receptionist I was from Channel 5, which had just conducted the interview. We thought our cameraman left a tape. She went to check the office, came back and said, 'Mr. Hightower says there's nothing there. Sorry.' So you know it's the right man."

"Cool. Thanks for the hookup! I just have to catch Zeke before he gets off and I'll be ready to roll. What's the address?"

The next thing I did was telephone Zeke and talk him into doing a sister a solid, help-me-do-some-catch-up work to redeem myself. Like En Vogue sings, "What a man . . . what a mighty good man!" He was ready to go.

But Fab Weaver's lawyer? Horace Hightower? That's another story. It turned out to be *drama* for this *mama*.

I linked up with Zeke at Mr. Hightower's office on Lasalle Street. The building that Hightower and Loeb is located in had a healthy buzz. A guard at the front desk called upstairs to the tenth floor and yes Mr. Hightower was still in and yes we could come up.

The outer office had carpet so plush I nearly lost my balance coming off the wobbly floor of the elevator. Domed lights shone brightly on the octagonal desk, behind which sat an elderly woman, salt-and-pepper hair cut flat and close like Liza Minnelli's. She wore oddly shaped eyeglasses low on her nose—large and Euro, like Beamer brake lights. "Ms. Barnett. Here's a statement from Mr. Hightower. That's what he's giving to reporters who request an interview."

Oh no, see, I can't be put off like that.

"But the man had a sit-down with Channel 5," Zeke said. "How come we get the high school cheat sheet?"

The receptionist's eyes smiled over the top of her glasses. "Mr. Hightower likes Channel 5."

I said sweetly, "As if your TV preference should matter in a murder case. Ma'am, can I just make the request of Mr. Hightower in person . . . ?"

"I'm sorry." Then she slid an open ledger to the end of the counter with a Mont Blanc pen. "Please sign that you have received the statement."

I looked over the list, scanned it briefly, saw the Hancock of Channel 5's reporter at the top of the page. Next I saw the signature of one other reporter, print, from the *Sun-Times.* I signed my name.

A young woman in a sweat suit walked past us, carrying a bunch of packages. She stood at the double glass door. "Delivery from the mail room."

The receptionist acknowledged her with a nod, then pressed a button beneath her desktop. The doors popped open and the woman walked through. Zeke took a step in that direction as the doors closed, managing only to look through them, glancing to the right. We saw a man walk past the door carrying a file.

"Sir, please come away from the door," the receptionist ordered sternly.

"But, ma'am." I began pleading my case. "If you could ask Mr. Hightower if he would see me for just five minutes . . ."

Ego trippin' her mind is slipping. Hightower's receptionist was loving the power of saying yes or no. Zeke didn't move away from the double glass door.

I pointed to the press statement. "Well, the very least you guys could do is put together a stronger press statement. Look at all the misspelled words."

"Where!" The receptionist grabbed the statement from me, scanning it quickly.

Zeke slammed his palm against a steel square emergency button. A sharp clicking sound and the double glass doors off to our left opened. Zeke turned his camera on and he was moving. I was right behind my favorite news cowboy! I ignored the receptionist's pleas.

There were two hallways, one left and one right. We chose right, shaking doors one by one. The receptionist was on our heels crackling like fire with me steadily calling, "Mr. Hightower!"

This place looked like dough. Big dough. Smelled of money. Looked like money. Made you wish you had gone into law so you could make some money.

"What's going on here?" a man demanded, opening his door. He was attractive in a rough way, extremely masculine. He had dark hair and eyes, broad shoulders, thick arms. Rugged chin.

"Georgia Barnett, Channel 8 News. We'd like to talk to you about the Fab Weaver murder case. . . ."

"I told her no, Mr. Hightower. I called Security!" the receptionist said, trying to defend herself.

"It's fine, Betty, fine." His tone softened and calmed her down. Then he stepped aside and invited us in. Horace Hightower was dressed like a high-priced lawyer, crisp tailored shirt and expensive slacks with a dense pleat down the front. His shoes were expensive— spit-shined with a tassel for a flea-flicker of personality.

Sorry to have had to do a job on Betty but I had to see this man. Mr. Hightower sat behind his desk after telling Zeke and me to have a seat. "Three questions, Ms. Barnett. That's all I will answer."

Three questions? He was ticked off. Tried not to show it.

"I hope you aren't upset about our little commando run; we just wanted to talk to you because we knew you would be a great interview."

"No, I'm not upset and your flattery is unnecessary. Now you have two questions remaining."

So those were the rules, huh? Hightower was underestimating me. I'm not just some tight skirt with my brains tucked into the hem. Please!

Zeke began setting up the interview shot.

"Can you hurry?" Mr. Hightower said and began flipping his pen up and down, allowing it to land with a thunk on a stack of briefs.

"You and Fab Weaver filed an order of protection against Jimmy Flamingo—for what?"

"Last week we had a meeting with Mr. Flamingo. We were discussing a lawsuit he was considering filing against my client. He became violent. He punched Mr. Weaver in the mouth, then came after me. If it hadn't been for Security, he might have murdered us both then."

"What could have happened in this office that day to make him react so violently—three questions maybe?"

Hightower smiled then chuckled before bowing his head a bit. "He was angry because we told him that his lawsuit would be fought every step of the way because Mr. Weaver did write and produce every song he's credited with. We haven't lost a challenge yet."

"Did Mr. Weaver—"

"That's three."

"This is the bonus question for getting you to break form a moment ago."

He nodded his approval.

"How much money has Mr. Weaver made on the songs that Mr. Flamingo claims he stole?"

Hightower eased back in his double-padded leather chair, stroked his chin, thoughtfully. He asked, "Can I estimate?"

"For another question, sure."

He smiled again, then sighed.

"I'd estimate somewhere in the neighborhood of two million dollars."

Damn! And Jimmy was behind on $500 a month rent. I shook my head, stared him in the eye, then raised my left brow.

"Something bothering you, Ms. Barnett?"

"I was just wondering if that two million included the licensing money for the use of one of Jimmy's songs in that new car commercial."

"Yes it does. That's it. Now thank you for coming—"

"I still have another question, sir."

"You just asked—"

"I didn't ask. I said I wondered. I wondered out loud and you offered the answer, Mr. Hightower."

Shoot, not only am I a reporter, my mama is a lawyer! Mr. Hightower had his hands full.

He rubbed his chin again. "Last question, then."

"Do you know where I can find Fab Weaver's son, Guy?"

"Guy Weaver is not stable. As the executor of his father's estate I don't feel that he should be questioned by the media."

"That's not what I asked you, Mr. Hightower—"

"That's my answer. My client, Fab Weaver, has been murdered. I didn't find out about it until I got back from vacation in Wisconsin. The man's body has been in the morgue unclaimed like he's some—some nobody pauper—"

"He's got family. Is Guy still coked out?"

"No comment. Listen, I have to look after Guy through Fab Weaver's estate and do you think he gives a damn? Absolutely not. I had to threaten to not pay his bills this month if he didn't go down to the morgue today and sign for the release of the body. I still have to make the funeral arrangements, so if you don't mind, and even if you do, please see yourselves out, Ms. Barnett."

Hightower was sweating now. I felt a twinge of remorse. I egged him on when he was trying to deal with the death of a friend while protecting the man's son. He'd just returned from vacation and had hit the mother lode.

Mr. Hightower stood up.

I got up and spoke sincerely. "I'm sorry about the death of your client. I know you've got a tough task ahead of you. Good luck and I hope after things settle a bit, we can sit down again for a follow-up interview."

Mr. Hightower relaxed. "Thanks and no thanks."

Then Zeke and I left.

"Now what, Georgia?" Zeke said, revving the engine.

"To the county morgue."

Chapter Eleven

DEATH'S EYE WAS ALWAYS OPEN AT THE COUNTY MORGUE. It watched as you came in.

Death's breath propelled you down the hall, cool crisp air to keep the bodies cold.

Death's heartbeat kept you alert, the sound of doors slamming behind empty bodies and vanished spirits.

Death's scent made you want to hurry up and leave; it was the bad odor of time running out.

Ju Wung told me on several occasions that he'd gotten used to having death around. He'd learned to ignore it like a spouse in a *cheaper-to-keep-her* marriage.

But of course, he was fifty-five years old and had worked in the morgue for twenty years. He took a liking to me when, during my senior year of college, knowing I was going to be a reporter and would find myself in a morgue at some point in time, I asked for a tour of the place.

Wung tried to scare me.

He tried to gross me out. At the time I gave him a black girl neck swirl with more snap than a rubberband. I told Wung, "I want to see everything. I'm going to be a journalist, you know."

The brashness of youth won me a place in his heart and him a place in my Rolodex of sources.

"Whatcha need, Georgia?" he asked, stabbing a square of lasagna steaming in a silver tin on his desk.

"Thought you were cutting down on those fatty foods and stuff. How are you feeling? Still fighting high cholesterol?"

"Feeling good and I'm eating Lean Cuisine!" Wung grinned. "Two of 'em on one plate, but still that's something."

"Crawl before you walk," I encouraged him. "Listen, I need some info. You had the body of a murder victim in here. Fab Weaver. His son Guy came in today to sign for the release of the body. I need his phone number and address."

Wung licked his fingers. He cocked his head to the left as if deciding whether or not to give me the information.

"Pretty please with sugar on top?"

Wung smiled. "That's why I love you, Georgia. You ask about my health and you say please. For a woman like you, I'd give the world. I'm thirty-five years old and still available."

I laughed.

"Oh that's funny?" He made a cartoonish, shocked face. "Don't you know? No one ages in the morgue. The age you come in at . . . is the age you stay. Started here when I was thirty-five, so I'm still thirty-five."

I looked around the dingy office, the old file cabinets, the three outdated computers. "If this is where you find eternal youth, your sister-friend will skip it!"

"Good choice." Wung shoved some food in his mouth then scooted his chair back with his feet. He opened a drawer and pulled out some papers that kept track of the morgue bodies.

"Guy Weaver," he said after swallowing, "signed a release for his father's body today."

I flipped open my pad and started writing down the address and phone number. I gave Mr. Wung a hug and reminded him about taking care of himself. Then I jetted back out to the news truck.

Zeke had a corned-beef sandwich and a Coke. He offered me half the sandwich. That's when I realized that I was starving. But I still had the smell of the morgue in my nostrils and the taste of it in my throat. Those two factors forced me to deny food to my cramping stomach. "No thanks, Zeke."

"That's why I didn't go in there. What now?"

I looked at my watch. Time was flying. I examined the information I had on Guy Weaver. I didn't want to call ahead, he might have caller ID and I didn't want to tip him off that I was coming.

I had just enough time to get back to the station and hand off Hightower's interview to Brent Manning's writer for the ten o'clock news.

Brent Manning was the news director's pet at WJIV. He was good, but not nearly as good as he thought. Arrogant. Combative. Funny-looking. Arguably the best reporter in town, he only got assigned to the top stories, and the Fab Weaver murder happened to be one.

If I'm lying I'm flying. It hurt my pride to have to field produce an interview for Brent like a college intern but team player is the name of the game in news. I had bigger issues than our battling egos. Brent could incorporate Hightower's interview into his 10 P.M. piece on Jimmy's arrest.

I asked Zeke to hand off the tape for me when he went inside to park his vehicle and get the assignment desk manager to sign off on his overtime. I didn't want to show my gorgeous girlfriend mug because it still, despite getting the interview, had *latte mocca* on it.

I went to my BMW and paged Doug. I punched in 911. Then I pulled out. My stomach growled. I needed to eat or I was going to pass out. I passed McDonald's and stepped on the gas—Mickey D's went to my hips faster than Doug's hands.

I saw one of those chi-chi-poo-poo delis on the corner—turkey sandwich with roasted tomatoes, six bucks. That's steep but to save a sister's life? Hey, like Marvin Gaye says, "got to give it up." I could barely get out of the car, nearly ready to fall down from fatigue.

I got my sandwich and had begun wolfing it down when my phone rang. "Hello?"

"It's me, Doug."

I was glad to hear his voice. But mad to hear his voice. "Doug, what's going down with Jimmy?"

"We've been questioning him. He says he's innocent."

"Well, you sound like you don't believe him."

"I didn't say that. I'm just trying to put all the pieces together. Some of it looks bad and some of it has holes in it."

"All right, run it down for me."

"Off the record? This is for Jimmy."

"Fine."

"Fab Weaver's attorney called us and said that an order of protection was previously filed against Jimmy. He threatened both their lives. Once we found that out, we tried to pick Jimmy up."

"Yeah, he was in that gambling hole where Peaches and I found him."

"You should have called me when you found him in that gambling hole. I keep telling you that you're too headstrong. A hard head can make a soft behind—except now it's Jimmy's behind."

"Hey, don't leave that baby on my doorstep. I wanted to call you but Peaches wouldn't let me."

"And man, is she ever clowning. She's been demanding to see Jimmy. We wouldn't let her talk to him even if he wanted to talk to her; keeps mumbling something about Peaches being bad luck."

"She's pretty pissed off with me. Thinks I tipped you guys off that Jimmy was at the hospital."

"Naw, a hospital nurse saw Channel 5's coverage and called in. I'll tell Peaches so she can stop tripping on you."

"I don't want Jimmy to get railroaded."

"Like I do? But the evidence is stacking up, Georgia. While we were checking out the bars and clubs that Jimmy hung out at, we picked up some head shots."

"Publicity photos and stuff?"

"Yeah. We got ahold of one of Jimmy and a couple of the other musicians. We brought Angelina Rosseni into the cop shop and asked her did anyone look familiar. She pointed out Jimmy. Said he was the one she saw threaten Fab Weaver in the yard that day."

"Aww, Doug, so Jimmy threatened him. I've told a boss or two that I was gonna kill 'em. And every last one of them is still breathing."

"But that wasn't the first threat. And besides, Georgia, we have a hell of a motive in this case. Jimmy says the victim cheated him out of millions. Jimmy threatened a lawsuit and they basically called him over to the law office and told him to eat shit and die."

"Yeah, took his money and then disrespected Jimmy on top of it. Okay, Doug, I'll give you that. It does look pretty bad. Now please, throw a sister a hope crumb. What about the holes in the case against him."

"Autopsy report shows scrapes on the back of the murder victim's hands. The wounds are inconsistent with a struggle. More like the body was dragged. And there were some fibers under his fingernails. Because of the autopsy we do know he was killed two days ago, Sunday, late. Sometime that night between 9 P.M. and midnight. But we don't know where yet."

"So you can't put Jimmy at any particular murder scene."

"Right. Jimmy says he was home alone asleep. There's no one to verify his story, so that's weak."

"What about the murder weapon? What's up there?"

"Fab Weaver was shot with a twenty-two. We had enough probable cause to search Jimmy's apartment but we didn't find any gun."

I sighed. "Well, that's something. I feel a little better."

"That gun is really key, Georgia. We all know Jimmy had a twenty-two."

"Yeah, Peaches told me he liked to tote it around in the waistband of his pants sometimes. I'm glad the other detectives don't know that."

"Yes, they do. See, I made Jimmy register it—saw him with the gun once. I told him he'd better register it. So we all know Jimmy owned a twenty-two. But when I asked him for it, he said somebody stole it from his apartment."

"Sounds like a lie."

"Doesn't it? But we don't have enough evidence to charge him, so we'll have to let him go in twenty-four hours."

"I want to believe in Jimmy."

"Georgia, if we could get our hands on that gun, we could rule out his weapon. That would help a lot. With Jimmy being our only suspect . . ."

"What about the victim's son, Guy? He's probably a dope fiend according to Mr. Martelli, who saw him throw a fit on his dad. And Horace Hightower, know what he says? He says Guy hates his dad but lives off the comfort he provides. So Guy could just as easily have gone on a drug binge and done something terrible too, right?"

"Our guys checked Guy Weaver out this afternoon. Said he was a piece of work, that he hated the old man, but they didn't get any indication that he was lying about where he was. Said he was at a meeting for recovering addicts the night of the murder. North Shore New Life Center. It checked out. Look. I gotta run."

"Okay, Doug, do whatever you can for Jimmy, please."

"I'll be fair, Georgia. Unless something breaks or he makes a drastic change in his story, I think we're going to have to eventually release him. But that missing gun is bugging me. But hey, you're off tomorrow, right?"

"Yeah, I took a comp day. Mama's on vacation this week and we said we'd spend some time together. But maybe I should work. I don't wanna miss anything on this story."

"Take the break. Go see your mom, get some home cooking. You've been running like crazy on this case and it's wearing you down."

"Maybe you're right."

"So pack it in, go home, and get some sleep. Promise?"

"Thanks, baby, I promise."

I did get some sleep eventually—after I made one more stop. I drove over to Guy Weaver's apartment, a high-rise building on North Lake Shore Drive. Daddy took good care of his son despite their differences.

The night air decided to get more like a Chicago winter, tight and very cold. I always kept a heavier jacket and coat in my trunk when the weather was unpredictable like this. Never knew when I'd have to do a live shot outside in *whatsomever* kind of weather. I'd learned to be prepared—saved me a slew of sick days and Alka-Seltzer Plus Cold Medicine.

I pulled the hat down on my head and flipped my collar up. Looking Pam Grier fine? I wasn't. Feeling Yogi Bear warm? I was. I walked into the lobby near the lakefront at Belmont. The doorman greeted me warmly; when you are on television people think you're a star. I wasn't feeling like one. My feet hurt. My eyes were beginning to burn from fatigue. But I asked the questions I needed to.

The doorman told me that he had not seen Guy Weaver since late in the evening. I gave him my card and twenty dollars. I promised him another twenty if he paged me as soon as Guy Weaver came home. Was he working tomorrow? Till 8 A.M., he said. I gave him another card and told him to give it to his relief man—and the same promise of twenty bucks for a page when Guy Weaver returned to his apartment.

Then, finally, I went home and crashed.

Chapter Twelve

AN ACHING BODY IN A COMFY BED WILL LULL YOU INTO A coma. I slept hard. When I did finally wake up it was almost noon. I had more creases on the side of my face than a basket full of dirty sheets.

I was starving and I knew where to go for a meal—my mama's house. Whether it's a Sunday or the middle of the week like today, Mama's got something good to eat in the house.

My mother lives in a rehabbed mansion in Hyde Park. She got the place for taxes twelve years ago and each year has done something major to improve it. It's about half a mile from the lakefront. Mama loves the lake. When we were struggling growing up and Mama was studying law in night school, she'd take us to Rainbow Beach to sun—but not much: "Get up under the umbrella before you get too black"—and we loved the smell of the water, the sound of the gulls, and the lure of the gentle waves.

It was now 1 P.M. I was almost at Mama's house, so I got myself mentally ready. My mother has a brilliant mind. She crafts a hell of a closing statement and can tell you off with elegant flair. Sometimes that last gift makes her a hard person to be around.

For example, when Mama sees you after you've done something to make her good and goddamn mad, she'll come up with a phrase to fit her anger. That phrase is then put behind the title of Mr. or Ms. *Who's bad!*

I knew I was gonna get it. Mama's mad at me—mad as a Sumo wrestler on Slim-Fast. I hadn't called or stopped by the house or office in well over a week. I knew she was on vacation and had promised that we'd spend some quality time together. When Mama opened the door, the first thing out of her mouth was, "Well, Ms. Long-time-no-see, how are you?"

"I know, I know," I said, trying to give her a big hug. Mama gave me a cheek and blew a kiss that touched more air than skin. Yep, she was pissed and going to put on an afternoon matinee starring the world's best-loved drama queen—herself.

"My, you've grown since the last time I saw you," she remarked, heading toward the kitchen.

"Give me a break. I'm practically forty—the only thing I'm still growing is hair under my arms."

I followed Mama into the kitchen and sat at the counter.

"Well, the only time I see Ms. Reach-out-and-touch-no-one is when she's on television."

"I've been working on this murder story like a dog the last couple of days. And then when it involved Jimmy . . ."

"I know, baby. Georgina has been keeping me posted." Mama hates the nickname Peaches. "I was worried to death about your sister. She gets so emotional. And Georgia, you know how crazy she is about Jimmy. We've known him for years. I can't believe he'd do something like that—drugs are one thing, but murder?" Mama shook her head, *oh no.* "Not our Jimmy."

"They don't have enough evidence to charge him. Doug said Jimmy would probably be released—"

"You didn't hear?" Mama said. "He's out. I heard it on the radio this morning. Then Georgina called and said she would be by after taking him home. She's supposed to come get Satch. I put him down for a nap after we had some breakfast."

A smirk crossed my face.

"What?"

"Nothing, Mama."

"Nothing, my behind. I know I told Georgina I wasn't going to continue babysitting Satch every time she says boo. But I gave her a break this round because she's trying to help Jimmy."

"Yeah, Peaches has been going nuts with Jimmy and this police mess."

"I know. That's why I didn't gripe about keeping Satch. We owe Jimmy. He really helped Peaches when she was having that problem with her confidence."

"Jimmy was right on time," I said, thinking how much he had helped my sister.

"*And right now Georgina isn't!* She's late as usual. That girl can be so inconsiderate. And she needs to spend more time with her son."

"Mama, you're too hard on Peaches. She's very good with Satch."

"She's good, but she could be better. That's why I'm going to make sure I'm the one who tells that boy about his name!"

"He's only three, Mama."

"I'm going to wait until he's old enough, of course. And it's not a scary story if it's told properly. I'm going to tell Satch that he's named after my grandfather, *his* great-great-grandfather Satchel, who was famous across tight and open spaces in the South for having magical feelings in his bones."

"Yeah but the part about the cut-off fingers is scary stuff. At least I thought so, Mama."

"Oh, Satch is no big 'fraidy cat. He's got courage just like old Satchel. He could feel things in his bones. My father talked about his daddy all the time. He told me Grandpa Satchel said he knew the first time he saw Grandma Emma that she was the one to marry, said he felt it in his bones and knew that she would give him two sons."

"I remember Granddaddy used to tell Peaches and me that story *waaaaay* back when. We were trying to catch lightning bugs on the back porch."

"To this day, folks down South talk about my grandpa Satchel. He felt a storm coming a full day before. He boarded up all his doors and windows, even kept the children out of school. The entire family sat in the cellar with the sun shining just as bright. Everyone else laughed, until the storm came and every other house was damaged but theirs."

"That's not the scary part though." I frowned.

"One day, the Klan decided that Grandpa Satchel was becoming too much of a hero to the colored people in the area and something needed to be done. . . ."

"Now you're coming up on the scary part, Ma."

". . . and he felt it in his bones that they were coming for him but he didn't leave. Grandpa Satchel knew that if they didn't find him at home, in his bones he knew that they would hurt his family and some of the other colored families too. So he went out in the woods to meet them and never came back. A white man that liked Grandpa Satchel told Grandma Emma that the Klan boys said he fought fiercely; that he died looking them in the eye. The Klan boys dumped his body in the river. Grandma Emma cried and cried, they say, and clawed away from the hands holding her by the waist and took off running."

"Headed for the river but she didn't find a thing," I jumped in.

"Not a thing, child. The next year she looked again. Nothing still. That third year there was a drought and the land was dry as dust and no one made crops that year. People were starving, getting sick, and the river had run dry. Grandma Emma went out in the woods again and this time when she sat beneath a tree to cry, her hand touched something. It was two bones, two cut-off bones from a human hand."

"Satchel's bones!"

"And Grandma Emma took those bones and wrapped them up in a white apron and buried them in the backyard in that dry, crusty ground and the next day . . . *the very next day* . . . there was a pool of water where she had dug. The other colored folks came and looked in wonder. Then they started to dig in a fit—with their hands, spoons, a shovel. They dug a well and that was the only water around for miles. Grandma Emma let anyone with a bucket get them some water—even some of the Klan whose children were now starving. She let them all drink from Grandpa Satchel's bones."

"I think my little nephew is going to like that he's named after Satchel."

"I think so too," Mama said.

The doorbell rang.

"Ahh, there's Ms. Contrary now!"

"I'll get it," I said, and went for the door. I opened it and there was Peaches, looking ragged and sleepy in a green sweat suit beneath a thick flak jacket. Peaches had on her favorite hat—it was a floppy knit number from the seventies—red and green crochet with a big white pompom on the top. Peaches made it herself when she was eight years old. She looked like a Fifth Dimension wanna-be. I teased her. "Lose the brim."

"Lose the 'tude." Peaches grinned at me. Then her voice dropped to a whisper. "Sorry about what happened at the hospital. I was tripping, you know?"

I hugged her. "I know."

Peaches cupped the back of my neck. "Still love me, sister-twin?"

"Yeah, but you sure make it hard sometimes. How's Jimmy?"

"Getting there," Peaches said, stepping inside the door, taking off her jacket. "Dropped him home. Wouldn't ride with me at first, still talking that nonsense about how I brought him bad luck."

"I guess riding in the car with bad luck is better than good luck on the bus."

Then we heard the rattle of pots in the kitchen. Peaches winced a bit. "Is Mama gunning for me?"

"Like the U.S. after a terrorist."

Peaches' shoulders just sagged, then she quickly brushed past me. As I entered the kitchen several steps behind her, I heard my mother's voice.

"Well, well, well . . ."

"Ma," Peaches said, leaning on the other end of the counter, "this is not the day for this, please." Peaches grabbed a piece of bacon off the breakfast plate Mama had made for me.

Now there were four pieces of bacon left as I sat down on a stool in the center of Mama and Peaches.

"Oh, don't serve me attitude this morning, Ms. I-couldah-called!" Mama grabbed a piece of bacon off the plate, crunching it back at Peaches.

Three pieces of bacon left on the plate.

Peaches took my bowl of grits. She took my spoon and started whipping the grits fiercely. "Sorry, Mama. Is Satch ready?"

"No, Ms. My-mama-ain't-got-nothing-else-to-do-but-wait-on-me!"

"Why not!" Peaches looked at her watch, then ate some of my grits. "I'm ready to go!"

"Then you should have gotten your butt here on time." Mama grabbed a piece of my toast and started eating it.

One piece of toast and three pieces of bacon left! I reached for a piece of bacon and Peaches grabbed it and crunched it in half and started using what was left as a pointing stick. "You did this on purpose just to start something."

"Mama, give her a break," I said, hoping that that would make Peaches leave at least a few spoonfuls of grits in the bowl.

"Stay out of this, Ms. Show-up-when-you're-hungry!" Then Mama said to Peaches, "You have to spend more time with Satch. He's starting to think I'm his mama and not you."

"Jesus, the boy ain't going crazy, is he?" Peaches snorted, showing me the grits in her mouth.

"Ugghhh! I hate that!"

Peaches opened her mouth and showed me the chewed-up grits and bacon. "Aggghghh!"

"Georgina! I know you have better home training than that!"

"Nasty dog," I sneered at Peaches.

"Troll," she shot back.

"Slouch!"

"Big mouth!"

"Your mama!"

"Just a minute here!" Mama huffed.

Suddenly Satch appeared in the doorway of the kitchen, groggy, clutching a chocolate-colored teddy bear with an eye missing. "Waked-ed-ed up!"

"Awww, look at Grandma's baby!" Mama said, running to swoop up Satch before Peaches could move. "Did the evil twins wake you up with all that noise?"

Peaches and I looked at each other and said at the exact same time, "Us!"

"Mama," I said, "you're spoiling Satch rotten."

"Grandma can't help it." Mama cut a wicked glance at my sister Peaches. "I'm doing extra duty."

Satch was rubbing his eyes now and looking like the cutest three-year-old kid in the world. He reached down with both hands and grabbed the last two pieces of bacon off the plate, stuffed them in his mouth, and grinned at me.

"What can I say, kid, you got it honest!" I told Satch, then leaned back in my chair. Just like I get those feelings in my bones, honest.

I looked at Peaches, girlfriend was zoning—staring off into space. I knew what she was thinking. Truth was, Peaches couldn't get her mind off Jimmy. And neither could I.

Mama reached for the last piece of toast—no way! I jerked that toast off the plate and stuffed the whole piece in my mouth. The crusty, dry edges crumbled and fell down the sides of my face.

"Georgia! Not you too."

"Funny Auntie!" Satch gurgled and then applauded.

I just got up from the counter, stood there, and chewed.

"Georgia . . ." Mama warned.

I shook my head violently and held up my finger, one minute. I swallowed, then opened my mouth, "See, Satch, all gone!"

"All gone," Satch repeated.

"All gone just like me!" I said and headed for the door.

Mama called after me, "Honey, we haven't even had a chance to really chat."

"Gotta go! Gotta go!" I laughed at my crazy family as I walked. I skipped out the door and slammed it behind me.

Little did I know that within the very next hour, there would be a huge break in the murder case. That break would lead me to Fab Weaver's son, Guy.

Chapter Thirteen

ASIEST TWENTY DOLLARS I EVER MADE!" THE DOORMAN said, taking the two tens, folding them over, and slipping them into his pocket. He adjusted the red bow tie of his uniform and grinned at me. "Apartment 23-13. Third door on your left off the elevator."

When I got home from my mother's house, I found that the doorman had left me a message saying Guy Weaver was in his apartment and that I needed to get there quick because he might decide to leave again.

I had my reporter's notebook in hand and my mini-recorder in my pocket. I knocked on the door and stepped aside out of sight of the viewfinder. The door opened.

A man stepped out wearing a dingy powder blue bathrobe. He had on brown leather slippers, and was standing on the backs. He had a puffy mop of charcoal-colored hair and thick, unruly eyebrows. His facial skin was raked by acne. His nose, broad and flat at the tip, flared as he jerked his head left, then right, spotting me. A thick Adam's apple bobbed as he swallowed hard several times.

"Hi, Guy."

"That's me," he said, a little slurred, a little surprised. "I know you?"

"You might. Do you watch Channel 8 News?"

"Awww yeah," he said, squinting. "You're dressed kindah casual today. And I'm buzzed too. But you're Georgia Barnett. Saw that story you did on my father."

I waited for him to upbraid me for portraying Fab Weaver in such a black light or storm back into his apartment and slam the door in my face. I basically had reported that his father was a heartless, ruthless crook. Period. That's what the facts showed. And I stood by every doggone word of it.

Guy gave me a wicked smile. "You missed the family angle—his only son hated his guts too."

I was stilled by his raw boldness.

Then Guy proceeded to walk back into the apartment, leaving the door ajar. This physical gesture was computed in my brain: Guy was giving me an opening. I dug it. I'd seen this before. Sometimes you run into a person who wants to talk but needs you to pull it out of him, to justify it for him. If you can't, he'll lock up tight on you. I've lost a couple interviews in the past like that. I'd have to work for this one but carefully.

I walked inside the apartment, slowly shut the door as I thought about my strategy. Guy was sitting on the couch now, his legs crossed at the ankles on top of a brass cocktail table. The rent here was expensive—two grand a month, easy. The furnishings were not. The couch, lamps, cocktail tables, and such were all a set, like the ones forever on sale while being energetically advertised on independent television stations.

I sat down next to Guy. He had a bottle of open scotch on the table and a sweaty plastic tumbler in his hand. He squeezed it so tight that I heard the plastic pop.

"Guy, I'd like to talk to you about your father."

"Why should I talk to you?"

"Why'd you let me in?"

"I wanted a drinking buddy. Can't get anybody over here to party." Guy started to get up. "Have a shot."

"No, thanks. Scotch is out of my league. And I'm working. But that's not why you let me in, is it? To share a shot with you? I don't think so. I think you wanted someone to talk with."

"Why should I talk to you?" he said with a challenge in his voice.

"The same reason you let me in. You've got something to say and I'll listen."

"Nobody wants to hear what I have to say."

"Am I not sitting here? Guy, at the door you said I missed something in my coverage, the family angle. You can fill in that piece for me and for the people across the city following this story."

"What'll I get out of it?" he said, taking another drink.

"Some relief from the anger you've got built up inside. Talking about your father will do that."

"That's what a head shrink is for. I've talked a blue streak to them, that's for sure. And it ain't done much good. Why would you be any better?"

"Because I'm not getting paid and I won't cut you off when time runs out. I'm not a friend that you can't get to come over because they've heard it all before. Someone like me won't judge you, Guy. I'll really listen."

"You'll listen all right, then make me out to be the bad guy because I hate my father. But he's the wrong one. Been wrong."

"I've got enough sense to know that parents aren't always right. They're people too. I'm not a judge. I'm a reporter. I just want to know what your life was like with your father to understand him better through you. Just talk to me, Guy. As much as you want, as little as you want. Either way it's no problem. I'm here to listen and help you tell people about your dad."

Guy nodded okay.

"Now, don't let this throw you off," I said taking my mini-recorder out of my pocket. "I'd like to tape our conversation so I can get all the facts right and understand everything correctly. If you get uncomfortable with it just tell me."

He shrugged indifference.

"At the door, you said you hated your father. Why?"

Guy laughed, still with his head down, shaking it wistfully. "My father was a mean bastard."

"What did he do that was so mean?"

"What didn't he do?"

"Guy, I need you to give me some examples. Like what?"

"Like stuff, okay? My father was just mean. He—he never liked anything nice."

"Can you give me one example? Like what?"

"Okay, like this. When I was a kid and I'd come home from school with a drawing of the sun and flowers, he'd hardly look at it and push me away. I'm a little kid. My father would say it was sissy to draw so much."

"All children draw pictures, Guy."

"Someone should've told him that. My father wanted me to be a tough guy like him. Intimidate people. Make them afraid. I remember once, we were in the car, on the way to a carnival downstate. Daddy had to make a stop, a business stop."

Guy's eyes lost their light as he traveled in his mind's eye to a place of the past, a place he was going to reveal to me, probably because he needed to, wanted to, had to.

"We stopped at the record company and three guys were hanging around outside. Teenagers. Cooling out. They were taking a break from recording. As soon as my father got out of that car, the laughter stopped. And I don't know, it seemed like the sun went behind a cloud just as they turned to face him, and I remember thinking, *Even the sun is afraid of him.*"

"What happened next, Guy?"

"My father started yelling at the musicians, slapped one of them in the mouth. He used to be a boxer, was quick with his hands, and he hit hard as hell."

"Did the man hit him back?"

"No. He was afraid. He was just a teenager, a skinny kid. Daddy wasn't big. But he was mean as hell and violent. One of the teenagers did manage to say something back to my father. He showed some courage, poor bastard."

"Why do you think he found the courage?"

"Could have been because there was a woman standing there, a pretty woman. I remember that. Maybe she was his girl, maybe he just wanted her to be, but he talked back."

"Your father didn't like that, I'm sure."

"He didn't. My father grabbed that kid by the throat and banged his head up against the wall. He fell and my father started to kick him in the ribs."

"He kicked him?"

"Like a football player going for a field goal, wild hard kicks. I remember the kid balling up in a knot taking it, had to bite down on a stick he had in his hand to keep from screaming."

"What were the other teenagers doing?"

"Just standing around watching. Like they were watching a play or something. I thought Daddy was going to kill him."

"What made your father stop?"

"He looked over at the car. The window was rolled down and I was crying. Just sobbing . . ."

The pain of Guy's memories seemed to flow endlessly while his hope for healing seemed stranded at a dead end. *And . . . and . . .* I thought as I waited several moments before prompting Guy. "Then what?"

"My father froze. The way he looked at me gave me the creeps.

He walked back over to the car, got in, and slapped me across the face."

"Fab Weaver just hit you and didn't say anything?"

"He said, 'Weak.' "

"That made it worse, didn't it?"

"Yes, but I didn't cry anymore. I saw that kid on the ground and our eyes met and something gave me strength. I stopped crying. Never again. No matter how my father might yell or beat up on me, I did not cry."

"A lot of people hated your father."

"Yes. And you wonder why after what I just told you—"

"Did your mother hate him?"

Guy sucked air and began fumbling in his robe pocket. He pulled out a rumpled cigarette package. It was empty.

"Guy, did she hate him too?"

He balled up the package and threw a line drive across the room, hitting the wall.

"Are you okay?"

"Yeah. Mama didn't hate him. She loved him but was afraid of him. Weird, huh? She was too afraid to say 'Stop,' or 'No,' or 'Enough.' Mama developed heart disease. Holding in that fear for so long probably aggravated it. She died while I was away at college, bastard cried like a baby."

"That shows he had some feelings. No one is totally bad, Guy."

He gave me a sarcastic look—like, *give me a break.*

"So you blame your father for your mother's death."

"Of course."

"For your unhappy childhood?"

"Of course."

"So Fab Weaver deserved to die?"

"Of course."

"Guy, did you kill him?"

He stared at me. Was Guy hiding something? Something criminal? I tried to read his face the way airport security x-rays luggage. I asked again, "Did you kill your father?"

Finally Guy turned away from me. He closed his eyes, and said passionately, "Yes, ma'am. Every night. Every night in my dreams."

"You seem very comfortable saying that."

Guy opened his eyes and looked at me. "I am—because it's true and because I didn't kill him in real life. I was at the drug rehab center the night my father was killed and plenty of people saw me."

That kind of an interview is a silver bullet that can kill any type of positive flow that you have. I quietly gathered myself, thanked Guy Weaver, and left the place. He was about as stable as a rocking chair. The terror inflicted on Guy by his father showed in every fiber of his being. I felt sorry for him. Guy was deeply hurt, but the question was, was he a killer?

I've said before that anyone was capable of murder, but were they likely to murder? Guy Weaver had demons. That was for sure. Maybe he'd been drinking and drugging, trying to get up the courage over the years to hurt his father.

I got in my car and took a minute to gather myself. Doug said his men interviewed Guy and he had an alibi. Said he was at a drug rehab meeting the night of the murder and it checked out. What was the name of the place? North Shore New Life Center. Yeah, that was it.

I used my phone to call Information, then I called the center to see if the director would talk to me. Later on, I would head over to Doug's to play him my taped interview with Guy Weaver.

"North Shore New Life Center?" a woman answered. "Can you hold a moment?"

Before I could answer, I was on hold. I squeezed my pen as I waited for the woman to come back. "I'm sorry for putting you on hold. How can I help you?"

"My name is Georgia Barnett, Channel 8 News. I'm looking for the director of the center."

"That's Jean Hopson. One moment, I'll transfer you."

"Jean Hopson," the woman answered when the call went through. "May I help you?"

"Yes, I'm Georgia Barnett, with Channel 8 News."

"Oh hello."

"Listen, I'm at Belmont and the lakefront, can be there in two seconds . . . can we talk?"

"Well, I was about to leave and—"

"Please wait. I'm almost there."

I hung up the phone. Sister-girl was not trying to be rude, but I didn't want her to get cold feet thinking about the subject matter while I was driving over there.

The North Shore New Life Center was nestled at the end of a dead-end street, four miles away from Guy's high-rise. The building, according to the dedication cornerstone, was donated by noted psychologist Dr. Albert Swimmer in 1985.

I rang the buzzer at the double front doors. It was a couple of minutes before a woman came walking toward me. She gave me a nervous smile. "Ms. Barnett, I'm Ms. Hopson. You look prettier in person."

As one of my best friends likes to say, *Friend of mine.*

"Thank you so much for the compliment and for waiting, Mrs. Hopson. Can we talk in your office?"

"Sure."

We walked up two short sets of steps to a floor with three offices—for the director, the assistant director, and the supervisory counselor—plus a bathroom.

Jean Hopson was meager in stature, barely five feet tall. She was very shapely though, wide hips, stout arms. She wore thick glasses that magnified large, comforting sage-colored eyes. And she had a luminous smile. There was a feeling of serenity about her, something that put you at ease. She took a seat behind the desk. I took the seat right in front of it.

"I'd like to talk to you about Guy Weaver, Ms. Hopson."

"Jean. Jean is fine. I'm not allowed to talk about the people who come here for support."

"You talked to the police."

"Well of course, they're the police *and* it was concerning a murder investigation."

"That's what I'm looking into as well, Jean. I'm investigating it for my television station."

She shook her head. "I'm . . . not sure about this."

"I doubt if I'll ask you anything that would breach any professional ethics code. I just want to verify what you told the police, which I in turn learned from them. So it's not like you're talking out of turn or anything. It's the police telling me your story, with you simply verifying it. See?"

"Yes, I see. I still don't think it would be a good idea."

"Ms. Hopson. I understand that what you do is very important. Believe me I am not one of those people who think counselors and social workers are degreed babysitters. When I worked in Cleveland one of my best friends ran a clinic there for drug abusers, so I know the hours you guys put in . . . the heart you put in . . . and the money that you don't get paid."

Jean smiled. Full steam ahead, baby, I thought, full steam ahead. "I would not compromise you by asking anything about a person's medical history or police record. I just want to verify some basic facts that the police have already gone over with you."

Jean smiled again.

But ughhhh, I don't think I like it!

"I'm sorry." She shrugged. "I'm still not completely on board with it."

Now I know I don't like it!

I leaned forward. "Off the record. Do you think Guy Weaver could have killed his father?"

Jean raised an eyebrow, "Off the record, no. I don't think Guy is a murderer. No."

"Then help him." I leaned back. "I just want to do all I can to make sure the right person goes to jail for this crime, Jean. Not the wrong person. Just a couple of questions and I'll be out of your way in a flash, how about it?"

She finally relaxed; a calmness that sometimes accompanies agreement took over her body. Jean leaned back, crossed her arms on the desk, then nodded.

"Guy Weaver was here at the center that Sunday from seven P.M. till a little after midnight?"

"Yes, he signed in. His group had a meeting first. Each counseling session is divided into a group of seven with an individual leader. After the regular two-hour-long meeting, we had a little party to decorate the Christmas tree in the lunchroom downstairs. Some of the counselees brought homemade ornaments."

"Guy Weaver was here the entire time. Couldn't have possibly slipped out?"

"As I told the police, I don't remember any chunk of time when Guy was not here. He's pretty lively sometimes."

"Fab Weaver, his father, was shot in the back and his body dumped in the lake."

"I know. We offered Guy special counseling. He turned it down, assuring us that he was fine."

That boy is anything but fine, I thought. I asked Jean again, "But you're sure Guy was here that night, all night?"

"If I didn't see him, someone on my staff did," Jean said. Then she stood. "I'm sorry. That's more than enough, I think. And I have to go."

And I was glad to get that. I waited until she got her coat. We would walk out together. We passed the lunchroom. There was a janitor in there wiping down the tables. The centerpiece of the room was the gigantic Christmas tree. It was a large, bushy, good-feeling tree with a variety of store-bought and homemade ornaments.

"Oh that's pretty!" I said, suddenly feeling the warmth of spirit that the holiday season gives.

"Isn't it though?" Jean said. "But wait. You've got to see it lit."

She went to plug in the tree and the speckled orange, red, and blue flashing lights set the bottom half of the tree aglow. The top half remained dark.

Jean walked over and fiddled with the cord. "Wilson, can you fix this?"

The janitor, an elderly man around sixty, wearing blue work pants and a gray flannel shirt, walked over. "It's busted. Just bought these lights. Well, we'll just have to take 'em back. Hope Guy kept the receipt."

"Why would Guy have a receipt?" Jean asked.

The janitor kept fiddling with the cord. "Well, the other box of lights wasn't working either. Guy was the one who went out and bought these."

"During the Christmas party?" I asked.

"Yeah, went right up here to the store," the janitor said, frowning at the cord.

"What time?"

"Uh, nine maybe ten o'clock when he left, around in there."

"How long was Guy gone?"

"An hour or so. Said he'd walk it because it was such a nice night for winter. Right up here to that twenty-four-hour drugstore about a mile and a half away," the janitor said. "I'll pick up some myself today. We'll just have to take these back later."

Jean looked at me. I looked at her. I asked both Jean and the janitor for their address and phone numbers in case I needed to contact them later. Then I headed for Doug's house.

Chapter Fourteen

GIRL, DON'T YOU EVER SLEEP IN?" DOUG SAID, YAWNING AS he answered his door.

He looked too cute in his burgundy satin pajama bottoms, bare-chested, hair tousled, eyes dreamy with sleep.

"Only with you!" I answered, and gave him a gentle yet super-sexy kiss on the lips.

"Talk to me," Doug said.

Then he pursued me passionately, and I accepted his soft, sweet tongue deep in the recesses of my mouth. Honey never tasted sweeter than his kiss.

I stepped inside the door and wrapped my arms around his waist and we kissed again, deep, long, bending my back, and I thought how much I'd missed his sensual touch over the last few days while being wrapped up in this case. Afterward, let's just say we'd have some *suckeying* up to do.

"Are you awake?" I whispered.

"Hmmmm-huh," Doug answered, thrusting his hips against me, "can't ya tell?"

"Good." I patted him on the butt and walked right past him. "I got a break in the case."

I heard *ping, thunk.* It was the door closing then Doug's head banging against it.

"Sorry to leave you hanging."

"It ain't hanging!" Doug smirked. "Do you ever quit working?"

"Not when I'm on a burn, baby! Listen, I just came from the North Shore New Life Center. Where Guy Weaver says he was the night of the murder? Well, check this out. The director? She told your investigators that Guy was there all night from seven until the party ended around midnight."

"Right. Want some java, baby?"

"Coffee? No. Doug boy, it's five o'clock in the evening. Have you eaten anything?"

"Been sleeping all day. I was out late working; helping one of my guys out on a stakeout. I'm running ragged between that and this Weaver murder case."

"Well, eat something."

Doug gave me the okay sign and I heard the refrigerator open.

"So, Doug, it turns out Guy wasn't there all night."

"No?"

"Get this," I said, letting my bones get mighty comfy on Doug's *come get down* couch. "The janitor says Guy left for about an hour— supposedly to buy some Christmas decorations."

"Not a lot of time," Doug said, coming to the couch with a cup of instant coffee and a big glazed doughnut.

"Don't do that to yourself."

Doug tore a bite out of the doughnut. "Not as sweet as you, baby, but it'll have to do for now."

He made me blush. Boyfriend likes to make me blush. "Really, Doug, why isn't that a lot of time? Do you know where the murder took place?"

"No, and still no gun either. He'd have to be precise and quick to kill his father and dump the body into the lake, then get back to the rehab center in about an hour. But it could be done."

"The lakefront is only about ten minutes away. And listen to the interview I got with Guy Weaver. This will blow you away!"

I took out my mini-recorder and played the entire interview for Doug.

As soon as it was over, Doug stood up. "This man I wanna see myself, eyeball to eyeball, down at the station."

"That's what I'm saying. He's the one you guys should be grilling. Not just Jimmy."

My pager began vibrating against my hip. *"Whooooo and Whaaaaat!"* I said, looking at the phone number.

"Work?" Doug asked.

"Who else?" I huffed out a hot stream of air and rolled my eyes, snuggling deeper into the cushions of the couch, trying to decide whether or not to answer the page.

Doug ran his hand along the inside of my thighs, I could feel the firmness of his touch, caressing but with such authority. "Might as well call in," he said, still massaging me.

I enjoyed the steady flow of his hands. "Why?" I was trying not to move, not even to make a phone call.

"I'm going to have the boys pick Guy Weaver up so he and I can have a little talk at the station. I'll be tied up the rest of the night. You know you're gonna wanna break the story that he's being questioned."

I leaned up and looked at Doug. "You can kill a mood."

"You too. Remember our exchange at the door?"

I gave him rapid-fire kisses, "Two-shay-bay-bay!"

Doug touched my cheek as he left the couch and called the cop shop, leaving instructions to have Guy Weaver picked up. He went to shower and dress.

I called the station.

"WJIV!"

"Clarice? It's me, Georgia."

"Been trying to hunt you down," Clarice said. "Where are you?"

"At Doug's place."

"Whatever you gettin', girl, order up two."

"I'm strictly business."

"And I'm Whoopi Goldberg—with a perm!" Clarice snickered. "Listen, I got a call I think you might be interested in."

"Nope. I've got something else I want to follow up on." I didn't want to get stuck developing some filler story for the late show because it was a slow news day.

"Fine. It's all about the Fab Weaver murder. I'll just page another reporter—say Brent Manning?"

"Girl," I yelled. "You better not do me dirty like that. You know he makes me ill! What is it?"

"That's better," Clarice said, enjoying the serious backpedaling I was forced to do. "Got a call from a guy who works for the electric company. Said he was working Sunday night. . . ."

"That's the night Fab Weaver was murdered."

"Right. He says he saw something that seemed a little odd. He wanted to talk to a reporter about it."

"That would be me."

"My choice for high office any day of the week!"

"Cool. What's his name and where can I find him?" Clarice gave me the info. "I'll come into the station, hook up with a crew, then head out from there."

"Great, I'll have a shooter ready for you."

"Also, after I talk to this guy I need to go to the cop shop. The police are bringing in Fab Weaver's son for questioning."

"Whoa, Georgia. You're catchin' more than a hooker at Mardi Gras."

"Thanks. This son of his is a piece of work, girl. Emotionally he's a powder keg and hated his dad. He could be a prime suspect and that'll take some of the pressure off Jimmy. I'll fill you in later. I've gotta roll right now. Bye, Clarice."

I knocked on the bathroom door. "Doug baby, I gotta go. I'll see you later. I'm sure I'll be doing my live shot outside the police station for the late show. Page me if anything happens before that time."

"Okay!"

Then I left.

It took me an hour to link up with my one-man crew, Cooper. He's not one of my favorite cameramen like Zeke, but he's still a good guy, steady hand, creative eye, and quiet by nature. Traffic was particularly heavy. The weather was still warm for winter and dry, a blessing in Chicago, where the temperature can get lower than your shoe size and the snow can get higher than your car door.

The man I was looking for was named Hank Slimmer. He said that he would be working on the Near West Side putting the final touches on an electrical system for the grand opening of a new library in the up-and-coming area.

My cameraman and I drove down the alley behind the library. We spotted two sets of trucks and five men working, three on the ground and two on the poles.

I got out. "Hank Slimmer?"

The man on the ground pointed up to a light pole flush left, then gave me a whimsical smile. "What'd he do to get to be on TV?"

"Nothing yet."

"Hey, Hank, TV lady wants to see you down here!"

A man wearing a thick wool jacket, a white helmet, and a tool belt that jingled louder than the cymbals in a blues band shimmied down the pole. He raised a pair of plastic goggles, took off a set of padded white work gloves, and smiled. "I'm Hank."

"Good to meet you," I said, shaking his hand. "Is there some-where we can talk?"

"Here. I can take a break for about fifteen minutes or so. But I'm not off the clock for another couple of hours. No lunch break today either. A state senator and the mayor will be here for the ribbon-cutting ceremony tomorrow. We've got orders to make sure every-thing is in A-one order."

"Gotcha," I said to Hank. "This is my cameraman, Rex Cooper. We can just set up a shot here with the trucks in the back-ground. . . ."

"Not a chance, lady!" interrupted the first man I'd spoken to upon entering the alley, who turned out to be the supervisor. "It'll look like we're goofing off. That'll be my ass for sure."

I shmoozed him. "No it won't. It'll be great publicity. I'll make sure I get you in a setup shot working and I'll even say that you guys are out here on the double to make sure the library grand opening goes smoothly. It'll be okay. Hank here might have some important info about a big story I'm working on."

"Geez, you mean I can be on TV too? How'se about the other guys?"

"Sure, not a problem."

The supervisor thought long and hard. "Okay. Civic duty. Sure . . . but no more than fifteen minutes, got it, Hank."

"Got it."

Cooper set up the shot of me interviewing Hank. In the fore-ground you could see the truck and two of the men loading and unloading cable from the rear.

"Hank, you called the station with some information you think might be helpful in the Fab Weaver murder case?"

"Right. I called the police station on Thirty-fifth Street, near the ballpark. I know a guy there, Sergeant Jerry Bella. I told him that I had some information on the case. Sergeant Bella just blew me off.

He hung up before I could finish. So I decided to call the media. The guy's not doing his job."

I wrote down the officer's name. "Okay, tell me. Maybe it wasn't as important as you thought."

"See, I'm a crime buff. I can tell when something's important or not. I read a ton of real-life crime novels. Plus I follow all the big cases in the papers and on the news. I like to see how they'll turn out, stuff like that."

"Sure. Well, I'm glad you called me, Hank. Now, what's so important?"

"Well, Sunday night, I was out near Manning Pier. It was around ten."

"You actually worked that late on a Sunday?"

"No. I was helping out on an emergency. I'd been dispatched to work on getting power back up to a neighborhood just about two miles north of the pier. Had a faulty line."

"Oh yeah, I remember seeing a short little story about that in our newscast. Brown-out. No power over there for about five hours."

"Right. Anyway, I didn't get a break or nothing, so hey, I decided to just kill the last half hour waiting in the truck by the water. Crank up the heat. I know a nice quiet spot near a clump of trees to camouflage the truck."

"Sure, sure," I said, helping pull Hank along, "just taking a break."

"Right, power was back on. So what the heck? It was kindah cloudy out that night, but every now and then there'd be a break in the clouds and the moon would peek out. I saw a car sitting in the lot there, the east lot of the pier."

"Anybody in the car?"

"Not at first. I thought maybe somebody had car trouble or something and left it."

"Okay."

"Then I see these two guys coming up from the short trail, near Manning Pier. They were walking fast and arguing."

"You heard them arguing even though you were inside the truck?"

"I couldn't hear them. But the one guy, the taller one, was waving his arms. Talking with his hands. He gave the shorter guy a shove. That guy gives him a bump back with his body. But he's got his hand in his pocket, see? Threatening like. He kindah motions with it."

"Was it a gun?"

"I don't know, I didn't get a good look because my phone rings. It's my girlfriend. I took a sec to tell her I can't talk. Then I look back over there and I see both guys getting into the car. The tall guy is the driver. The shorter guy with his hand in his pocket is on the passenger side. They start burning rubber to get out of there!"

"Sounds suspicious."

"That's what I was trying to tell Sergeant Bella. I saw something odd. He wouldn't listen. Bella sucks on Tootsie Pops like Kojak, can you believe what a character he is?"

"Hank, could you ID the men from the pier if you saw them again?"

"Naw, from the vantage point I had, I didn't see their faces."

"What about the car?"

"Red Cavalier, like I got except mine is silver with a spoiler. After hearing about the body being found at Manning Pier the next day, I couldah kicked myself for not following them and trying to write down the plate number. That's what I shouldah done."

"That would have been a big help."

"But I know this. It was a rent-a-car." Hank smacked his gloves together confidently. It was as if he was applauding himself. "I know that for sure."

"How?"

"When it was pulling out, the car was moving pretty fast. But it slowed to make that steep turn there onto the drive. Know what I seen? There on the trunk was a big bumper sticker. It said Rent-a-Buggy with the phone number. That's the new rent-a-car company with the funny commercial."

"Oh yeah." I almost laughed thinking about the company that used clips from old westerns, raggedy stagecoaches rolling down prairie roads, before dissolving to one of their cars, touting their traditional service and their cut-rate prices. "Cute commercials."

"Yeah—think it's anything?" Hank said anxiously. He was quite a crime buff. He seemed eager for confirmation that he had an eye for crime.

"Sure. It's odd that the car was there. It's in the right place—Manning Pier. It's around the right time—Sunday night. And both those men were acting suspicious. And listen, even if it's not directly connected to the murder, maybe the two guys in the car saw something. Who knows?"

"Hey Hank!"

He waved at his supervisor then turned back toward me. "I knew it. Told that know-it-all flatfoot I had something."

"Thanks, Hank, I think I've got what I need. I appreciate the call. Let's exchange info in case you think of something else or I need to talk to you again."

We exchanged info, then my cameraman got shots of the electrical crew at work. I would be true to my word and include them in my story some kind of a way. Maybe Hank had something. Maybe he didn't. What he saw did sound odd.

My cameraman and I got back in the news truck. We began heading over to the cop shop. I wanted to find out the latest on Guy Weaver and his interrogation. I'd also try to call this Sergeant Jerry Bella and track him down, see why he hadn't bothered to follow up with Hank.

"Sergeant Jerry Bella," I said into my phone, now back in the truck on my way to the cop shop.

"Bella's gone for the day. This is Officer Greer. Can I help you?"

"Yes, this is Georgia Barnett, Channel 8 News. I need to talk to Sergeant Bella right away. I'm working a story and one of my sources is a friend of his and I need to verify some things. Can you help me?"

He did a solid for a sister, calling Bella at home and passing along my phone number inside the news truck. Sergeant Bella called within ten minutes. Basically, he said, Hank was always calling the station with ideas about who committed what high-profile crimes. Sergeant Bella said that he was harmless but a pest, so he hadn't bothered to find out exactly what Hank wanted after all, since he called with something "urgent" every other week. Sergeant Bella never calls him back.

I thanked Sergeant Bella for the heads-up and hung up the phone. My gut said that Hank was an eager beaver, but a liar? Naw.

My next move was to call directory assistance and ask for the phone number for Rent-a-Buggy. I ran the commercial in my head—they were new and they were cheap. The operator said there were only two locations in Chicago. One at O'Hare Airport. And one at Midway Airport. I dialed the one at Midway, since that was the closest location to the cop shop, our ultimate destination. The line was busy.

"Coop," I said, "what time is it?"

"'Bout eight-thirty," he said, looking at his watch, firing up the news truck.

"Can we make it to Midway at Fifty-fifth and Cicero, then over to the cop shop, and still have enough time to turn a piece for the ten o'clock news?"

"Nope."

Doggone it! If I wouldah had brah-man Zeke with me, we'd be hot-rolling it to the airport now—wouldn'tah had even had to ask. But hey, check this lead out now or later? Can't jeopardize the other

aspect of the big story, the true-without-a-smidgen-of-a-doubt
lead that Fab Weaver's son was being questioned about the murder.

Can't miss my airtime either.

But then again: no guts, no glory!

"Let's try it," I said and we slowly began pulling out of the alley.

"Dude," I said to Cooper with a laugh, "whatcha got your right
foot on?"

"The gas pedal."

"Oh. Thought it was a snake or something, you seemed scared
of it."

He picked up the pace. Where's Zeke when you need a speed
demon? At home, enjoying his evening, like this sister-twin should
be. Yet I couldn't be. This murder case was getting some juice and I
couldn't afford to miss nary a squirt.

Thank God the traffic heading to Midway Airport was easing up,
not as heavy as earlier in the day. We made it there in about thirty-
five minutes. We parked in the taxi section, taking journalistic liber-
ties as we usually did in the media, and I hightailed it inside. I passed
Hertz, Dollar, Avis. At the end of the plaza was Rent-a-Buggy.

It looked cheap too. The counter was smaller than those at the
other rental companies and there was a cheesy-looking chalkboard
with a couple of specials scrawled across it.

At the counter, there was a line of about six people. The two people in the very front were fussing their butts off at a young man glar-
ing at his computer screen. He had the studious look of a college
man, round spectacles, fade haircut, slim build, very neat, white
shirt and tie. But his face looked like it was on fire! Red from the
veins pulsing in his neck up to his temples.

I knew I had to cut the line. If I was anyone else? If I wasn't a television reporter? I'd be shot down with stares as powerful as bullets
or cut off at the knees by words flying off lips like daggers aimed at a
bull's-eye.

I was met with a simmering disdain, explosive murmurs of revolt. Luckily for me there was enough curiosity among the impatient and unhappy mob about why I was there to give me the maneuvering room I needed.

"Hi. I'm Georgia Barnett, Channel 8 News."

"Hi, I'm Malik, assistant manager."

"And he's slow!" someone from the rear of the line yelled.

We both refused to turn around and look. "Listen, Malik. I've got a news emergency here. I need to find out who rented one of your cars and when. It's like a puzzle. Can you help me find the information I need?"

"We're not supposed to . . ."

"He can't do anything!" a man in the front of the line whined. He was about forty-five, looked very military, high-top haircut, gray all over, ruddy red skin, tight muscles, neat pressed blue khakis and a white shirt under a black bomber jacket. "Me and my wife have been trying to get a car now for over an hour. Small but quicker and cheaper—some bullshit motto they've got! And this guy, geez-louise!"

A collective groan went up from the front to the rear of the line and back again; a vocal *wave* if you will, highly seasoned with animosity.

Ganging up on my man Malik. Bad move. He cocked his head to the left and looked at me, speaking louder than he should have or even needed to: "Sure, Ms. Barnett. I can take the time to help you. It *is* an emergency."

Curses bounced off my back. Cooper turned on his camera and said, "You all want to look like bad people on TV or good people?"

Vanity thy name is television wanna-be! They straightened up like a Christian choir. I put the rush job on Mr. Malik. "The car was a Red Chevy Cavalier."

"Plate?"

"Don't have a plate number. How many red Cavaliers do you have in stock?"

"At this location? Or at O'Hare too?"

"Both."

He typed with two fingers. That was problem number one. Then he was squinting.

"Glasses?" I asked.

"Contacts. Lost 'em."

Problem number two.

"We have eight Cavaliers all together."

"*Red* the lady said, you rocket scientist!" one of the disgruntled customers shouted.

"The more you harass," Malik said in a singsong voice, "the slower I will get. Red . . . there are three."

Okay, I thought. Now we're getting somewhere. "What are their plate numbers? Call them out and I'll write them down."

Malik started calling out the plate numbers.

"C'mon," a woman at the end of the line moaned, "is this for real?"

I jerked around. "Sorry. I'm working on a murder case."

That settled the crowd, *for the moment.*

"Now, let's check the first plate." I looked at the notes I had scribbled. "Let's try Bug 677."

"Car," Malik said, reading the screen, "is still out. Been out for three weeks now. Allstate is picking up part of the rate, the customer is getting his van fixed."

"What's the name?"

"Burton Hallic . . . address . . ."

I wrote it down next to the plate. "Okay, try this one. Bug 313."

"The car was rented to Guy Weaver . . ."

"What?"

". . . rented to Guy Weaver," he read slowly, "charged to his Visa credit card account . . ."

I wanted to shout. I wanted to get the Holy Ghost. I scribbled down the info. "That's it. Is the car in or out now?"

"It better be out!" the man at the head of the line growled. "He just told me he didn't have any more midsize cars. I think I'm going to kill somebody in a minute."

Malik straightened his tie then turned to me. "And it was never returned. The car was reported stolen. That's part of the reason why we're short on vehicles today."

"Thanks, Malik. I appreciate it. Can you leave the screen up?"

Cooper came around the counter and got an over-the-shoulder shot of Malik at the computer with the screen showing the key information I'd just gotten.

No rest for the weary. We bolted for the cop shop. When we got into our news truck I called into the assignment desk. "Clarice? Me. Georgia."

"Hey you!" she said in a scolding tone. "What's your location?"

"Leaving Midway—"

"Midway? You didn't tell me you were heading to Midway. What for?"

"That lead you gave me is popping, girl. Hank the electrician? He said on the night of the murder that he saw a strange car at Manning Pier. Next day that's where Fab Weaver's body is found."

"Yeah? Shit, well, how'd you get to Midway?"

"It was a rental. Rent-a-Buggy."

"Oh yeah, G. I like that TV ad—it's one of my favorites, behind the brothers' *Whatz Up!* beer commercial."

"Well, there's nothing cute about who rented the car—that's now missing I might add. It was Guy Weaver."

"Jamming!" Clarice grunted. "We've got some kick-butt stuff on this story now. What's your next move?"

"I'm gonna try and write some of my story while we drive to the cop shop for the ten o'clock show. Anything new there?"

"No. It hasn't crossed the news wires yet that Guy Weaver's been brought in for questioning. None of the other stations are teasing any new developments on the murder case. I think we're all good. I think we've saddled an exclusive."

I felt so good I wanted to slap myself five—instead I grinned to myself and hung up the phone.

Chapter Fifteen

GOOD EVENING. I'M GEORGIA BARNETT, STANDING BY LIVE at Area 12 police headquarters. Channel 8 News has learned exclusively that the son of record producer Fab Weaver is inside being questioned about the murder of his father. That is just one of several crucial developments that have occurred within the last twenty-four hours."

Take the tape with natural sound up full:

Guy Weaver yells at the camera as he's being walked from one interrogation room to another.

"I didn't do anything!"

My taped narration begins:

"Guy Weaver says he is innocent. The forty-year-old North Side man was brought in for questioning this evening. He admittedly had a rocky relationship with his father and often dreamed about killing him."

**TAKE MY Q&A WITH GUY WEAVER/
FREEZE WALKING SHOT OF HIM,
PLAY AUDIO FROM MY MINI-RECORDER:**

"So you blame your father for your mother's death."

"Of course."

"For your unhappy childhood?"

"Of course."

"So Fab Weaver deserved to die?"

"Of course."

"Guy, did you kill him?"

"Yes, ma'am. Every night. Every night in my dreams."

My narration begins again. File tape of Fab Weaver's body at Manning Pier.

"On Monday afternoon, Fab Weaver's body was pulled from Lake Michigan. The coroner's office determined that he had been shot to death the day before sometime between 9 P.M. and midnight."

CUT TO VARIOUS B-ROLL SHOTS
OF THE REHAB CENTER.

"Guy Weaver told police that he was here at North Shore New Life Center that night, at a tree-trimming party for recovering addicts."

Under video Guy's voice:

"I didn't kill him in real life. I was at the drug rehab center the night my father was killed and plenty of people saw me."

MORE VIDEO OF THE CENTER.

"But along with police, Channel 8 News has learned that he did leave the party during the night, right about the time his father was murdered. He allegedly went to buy lights for the Christmas tree."

CUT TO B-ROLL OF ELECTRIC CREW WORKING.

"On the Near West Side a member of this electric crew called in a tip that may be key to the case. While out on an emergency call the night of the murder, Hank Slimmer saw a strange car parked at the very pier where Fab Weaver's body was later recovered."

TAKE SOUND BITE OF HANK SLIMMER/WITNESS:

"Then I see these two guys coming up from the short trail, near Manning Pier. They were walking fast and arguing."

CUT TO SETUP SHOT THAT SHOWS
ME TALKING WITH HANK.

"Hank says that the two men continued arguing as they sped off in the car. That car has now become crucial to solving this baffling murder mystery."

CUT TO VIDEO OF RENT-A-BUGGY
AT MIDWAY AIRPORT.

"The vehicle was a rental, from an independent company called Rent-A-Buggy. The red 2000 Cavalier had the license plate number Bug 313. When we at Channel 8 News tried to track down the car, we found out two interesting facts."

STOP AND TAKE SOUND BITE OF MALIK
EDWARDS/RENT-A-BUGGY CAR AGENT:

"The car was rented to Guy Weaver...charged to his Visa
credit card..."

**CUT TO REVERSE SHOT OF ME LISTENING.
BACK TO MORE MALIK SOUND BITE:**

"...And it was never returned. The car was reported stolen."
Dump tape. Take me live at the cop shop.
"Police are now looking for that missing car. Again
it is a red 2000 Chevy Cavalier license plate Bug 313.
Police plan to continue questioning Guy Weaver about his
father's murder, and with these latest developments, now
say he is officially a suspect. I'm Georgia Barnett live
at Area 12, back to you in the newsroom."

I FINISHED MY LIVE SHOT. WHILE COOPER PACKED UP THE
gear, I eased around the side of the cop shop to the parking lot, east
corner door. It was used by the officers who liked to take a break and
have a smoke. Just as we had worked out, there was Doug leaning
against the wall, waiting for me, sipping a can of Dr Pepper.

"Hey," he smiled. "Nice job on your news story."

"Yeah, I've been hustling all day, so much for rest and relax-
ation."

"I forgot to ask earlier, how's your mom?"

"Mama's a trip as usual, saw Peaches for a minute too."

"Yeah? How's she doing? And Jimmy too?"

"Peaches said that Jimmy was moody as hell, but physically he's
recovering very well. And she's not mad at me anymore, but she
looked very tired. I'm going to stop by her apartment before I go
home."

"Georgia, let grown folks be grown folks."

"What?"

"You heard me. Let grown folks be grown folks. Jimmy and Peaches will be fine. We can't clear him as a suspect yet, but at least Guy Weaver is on the hook too."

"Think he'll confess?"

"No. Swears he didn't kill his father. That he doesn't know anything about the car rental, claims the credit card was lost."

"Well, did he report it lost?"

"No," Doug answered, "says he meant to but never got around to it. Look, Guy Weaver's got a motive. Then a car rented in his name is spotted in the area the night of the murder just a few feet from where the body is later found. Guy had a window of opportunity. And he admitted he hated his father and wanted to see the man dead."

"Now he's the main suspect."

"Guy is in there sweating like a pig on Easter. By the time we get through grilling him, he'll tell us *everything*, including who he got funky with on prom night."

"Guy had help," I said. "Remember Hank Slimmer said he saw two people in the car that night. They probably had just finished dumping the body then. Wonder who he got to help him?"

Doug sipped his pop and swallowed. "Could be anybody. Especially since Guy Weaver used to be heavy on the get-high scene. A druggie will do just about anything. Ran Guy's name too. The man has four arrests for possession, one for petty theft. Lawyers managed to get him off."

"His father wasn't doing him any favors by keeping him out of jail. That just made it easier for Guy to keep *doing the do*, huh?"

"Really. Needed to give him some tough love, Georgia, some tough love. Say," Doug said suddenly taking my hand, "wanna help a detective out?"

"Of course."

Doug reached into his pocket, pulled out a set of keys. He placed them in my hand, then kissed it. "Go over to my place. I'll be home about midnight. Run me some nice warm bath water, lots of bubbles, *you know, just how you like it.*"

"Sure," I said, smiling, "I'll even put a little rubber ducky in the water for you."

"Now where would you get a rubber ducky this time of night?"

"That's for me to know and you to find out."

Two hours later Doug knelt by the tub, tracing the outline of a yellow ducky nestled above the bath bubbles that hit my shoulder at my breast line. He used two fingers as he traced, barely brushing the skin as if he were creating the image with magic oozing from the tips of his fingers. The warmth of the water massaged the small of my back and my hips. Coupled with that, his tracing gave me a tingling sensation in the pit of my stomach and in my throat.

The bathroom was dark except for the scented candles around the back of the tub, at attention on the ceramic ledge there. The smell of crushed roses filled the air along with the remembrance of intimate touches and understanding that only two bodies in need and in want of each other can communicate freely.

Doug wore a towel.

A red towel around his waist. A waist so muscular that the towel wrapped one and a half times, lying as flat as it would on the rack against the wall. The ripples under Doug's pecs were like a stream at sundown; slight in motion, welcoming the change from day to night.

Our change was coming, from cop and journalist to lovers.

I'd stopped by the twenty-four-hour drugstore, in the children's section, where I'd been last week buying my nephew Satch a game that helps teach children their letters. Next to the games, I spotted a package of temporary tattoos. The instructions said that they could be easily transferred to the body with water and by rubbing with a penny. Satch wanted a pony on his left cheek and a bunny rabbit on his right cheek.

Tonight when I bought a package for me, I wanted the cute yellow ducky between my breasts. Now a line of sudsy water was keeping it afloat.

Doug's fingers pressed harder, getting the ducky wetter and wetter. The suds enveloped his fingers as my body slid deeper into the tub. His fingers softened in the water as if they were melting against my skin, becoming my skin. My eyes told him to get in and he did.

The water reacted violently to the shift of power, but soon settled into balance. The balance of Doug's body against mine, finding comfort and space in our limited surroundings though intense with need and emotion.

Doug kissed my neck and I slid my hands down the sides of his hips. I squeezed and petted as he kissed and sucked my neck until I felt the blood rushing up my spine.

I shifted my body hard to the left, freeing up a sliver of space as the water splashed, slamming against the floor, dousing one candle. Doug filled that space with the front of his body as he moved up and down; the motion of the water and his skin made it feel like an oil slick was erupting down the middle of my body. The oil slick kept getting wider and slipperier. I closed my eyes and the room was completely dark except for the light of feeling glowing inside of me; a light expanding and illuminating along with the groans of passion that Doug gave.

My favorite part of our bath is drying, the expected yet unpredictable shivers Doug experiences as I towel off his body. If I touch Doug's back, the muscles in his thighs may shiver. If I touch his neck the muscles in his stomach may shiver. Like lightning striking, his sensual tremors are passed on to me through the faintest of touches, making his pleasure all the more fulfilling for me, and mine, for him.

Sleep afterward comes easy, like snow falling from the sky in soft, full puffs. We breathed as one, sinking into the rest and comfort of each other's presence. This murder case had temporarily stolen so much time from us it was a low-down dirty shame.

It was not the sudden burst of wind that shook the loose pane in the top bedroom window. No, we were used to the sound of that rattle, like car keys falling on a hardwood floor.

It was not the burst of the early-morning sun too bold through the window, laying its head against the pillow next to ours, no not that.

It was the shrill ring of my cell phone on the nightstand that woke us up.

It took me a few seconds to recognize the voice. Must have been because of the panic that was pulsating through every spoken timber. "This is Bang."

"Hey, Bang," I said. "What's up?"

"Georgia." Nerves broke his voice, his breathing was strained but was anything but under control. "I need your help. It's Jimmy."

"Jimmy?" I said, getting Doug's attention.

He stirred then grunted, "Damn Jimmy. I need some sleep."

"What about Jimmy?" I gripped the phone tighter, and shook Doug with my other hand.

"He's here," Bang said, "at my apartment up over the Game Room. We went down to the bar for a drink. I was trying to calm him down. Jimmy's been all upset and talking loud. He's acting all crazy, saying he's gonna leave town."

"Jimmy can't go anywhere, he's out on bail."

"I know that. That's why I'm calling you. Jimmy is out of control."

"Can't you take him home?"

"Every time I try he starts acting crazier. I can't calm him down. Don't make sense to drop him home in this state—he'll just go back out. No telling what Jimmy might do."

That gave me a chill.

"Georgia? Did you hear me?"

"Yes."

"Jimmy's high and wants to get higher. I can't find Peaches. I was hoping that you could come and talk to Jimmy. Keep him from doing something stupid."

"Just keep him there, Bang, okay? I'm on my way."

"How long you gonna be?"

"Not long. I'm hurrying. I'm gonna bring a friend with me, a police friend. Just stay with Jimmy." Then I hung up the phone.

Doug was salty about having to get up out of his comfy bed, that's for sure. I let him vent and told him the faster he moved, the faster we'd get back to bed.

It took twenty minutes for us to get to the Game Room. It was eerie. There was one light on, a naked bulb, sky blue, swinging by a frayed cord just over the bar area. The rest of the place was dark. There was only one other sliver of light glowing beneath the gap under the closed bathroom door.

Bang let us in. "I'm so glad to see y'all. C'mon. C'mon."

"Bang, this is Detective Doug Eckart."

"Sure, sure," Bang said excitedly. He was wound tighter than a poor whore's hair weave. "Jimmy locked himself up in the bathroom."

"Jimmy!" I called, walking closer to the door. "It's Georgia. And Doug. Come on out so we can talk."

There was no answer.

Doug drew his gun.

"What are you doing?"

"Georgia, I don't take chances, baby. As much as we both like Jimmy, he's still a murder suspect. You stay behind me. Try again to get him to come out. Go ahead. Call him."

We walked closer to the bathroom door.

Bang remained behind the bar, crouched a bit.

"Jimmy!" I called again. "Come on out so we can talk, okay?"

Still there was no answer.

"Jimmy," Doug called, moving closer to the door. "I don't want any trouble with you, man. You know that. C'mon out, please."

Still there was no sound.

"Step aside, Georgia."

I moved clear over to the wall. Doug took two short strides and kicked the door just a few inches below the lock. It popped off the hinges like a tree struck down by an ax.

The ball of light, once contained, burst into the room, nearly striking me blind. I fought to refocus. Then I saw Jimmy, lying on the floor. His head was turned flush left, snot running from his nose. "Oh my God!"

Bang was now at my side, clutching my arm. "He's dead. Aww, God! Jimmy's dead!"

Chapter Sixteen

DOUG DID NOT LET JIMMY DIE.

He pushed Bang and me away as he rushed to Jimmy's side. Doug felt his neck before flipping Jimmy over on his back. The quick motion jostled Jimmy's limp body and a gun came tumbling out of his pocket onto the floor.

Our collective awestruck gaze was like a spotlight. The gun spun around twice before coming to a dead stop.

"Oh shit," Bang said, leaning toward the gun.

"Don't touch it," Doug barked. "Call an ambulance!"

Bang ran back over to the bar, reached down, pulled up a black telephone, and began calling for help.

Doug delivered two open-handed smacks to Jimmy's chest, causing his eyelids to flutter slightly. "C'mon, man," Doug said as he began to administer CPR.

I've got a praying spirit, so I was on my job too, whispering the Lord's Prayer.

"He's breathing!" Doug huffed.

"Thank God!" I heaved and something drew my gaze back to the gun. "Tell me, Doug," I said closing my eyes. "Tell me that's not a twenty-two?"

Doug didn't answer me. He just continued working on Jimmy

until the ambulance arrived. Bang and I hovered near, watching and hoping. When the paramedics took over, Doug pulled out a hand-kerchief and delicately scooped up the gun. He, Bang, and I all fol-lowed the ambulance to the hospital.

"C'mon, Jimmy," I kept saying in the car. "Pull through."

Bang sat motionless with his head down.

Doug was stealth-flying behind that ambulance, dodging other vehicles, laying on his lights and siren. They took Jimmy right into the emergency room. We waited as they tended to him. Sadly we found out from the paramedic that Jimmy had lapsed into a coma on the way over to the medical facility.

I was weak with tension and fear; fear that Jimmy might die. Instinct kicked in and I paged Peaches because she knew Jimmy's family so well. He had a niece I knew about and an elderly mother. A blood relative needed to be there in case a major medical decision had to be made.

Bang was slumped in a chair, his mind probably roving back over the many years of friendship that he and Jimmy shared.

Doug sat next to him. "Bang, tell me exactly what happened."

"I don't wanna say nothing, man. Jimmy is my friend."

"If he's your friend, Bang, you'll tell the truth."

"I don't want to get him into any trouble. Jimmy was talking non-sense."

"Damn it, Bang, let me be the judge of that!"

Bang dropped his eyes, then glanced back up at Doug. "Jimmy, he—he, came here all upset. Said that he needed help, that he needed some money to get out of town."

"Why?"

"Don't make me do this, man," Bang said, agony distorting his face.

"Tell me," Doug said through clenched teeth.

"Jimmy said he killed Fab Weaver, him and the man's son."

"He and Guy Weaver were in on it together?"

"According to Jimmy. He said that the kid rented a car, got his old man to go for a ride. Jimmy shot him in the back. Then together they took his body to the lake and dumped it."

"Bang, did he say why he decided to run now?"

"Jimmy said that he thought Fab Weaver's son wouldn't be able to hold up in jail. Thought for sure he'd get scared and trick . . . and since Jimmy was the trigger man, he'd get the death penalty and the kid would get off light."

"Was Jimmy doing drugs when he came into your place?"

"Yeah, man, he was high when he got there. And getting higher every minute. Jimmy went in the bathroom to get a hit. That's when I called Peaches. Couldn't get her. Then I called Georgia. Figuring they could talk to Jimmy 'cause I couldn't do nothing with him."

"Did you give Jimmy any money?"

"No, man. Why would I wanna get mixed up in some shit like that? I'm too old to go to jail. I had enough trouble when I was a young man. I don't need any more trouble."

Then Bang put his head in his hands.

"Okay, Bang, okay," Doug said, patting his leg. "I hear you."

I went and sat next to Bang and rubbed his neck. "You did what you could. Now we just have to hope that Jimmy'll pull through."

Doug had already notified the cop shop about all that had happened. He and Bang went to police headquarters so Bang could make an official statement. Doug took the gun in. Ballistics would run tests to determine if it was indeed the gun used to murder Fab Weaver.

A little while later Peaches arrived with Jimmy's niece. His niece was about twenty-three years old, worked as a paralegal downtown, and seemed like a nice kid, going to school trying to make a way for herself and her young daughter.

Both she and Peaches came in wide-eyed and shaking. When a little something goes wrong, Peaches gets very upset. With something like this, she's a nervous wreck. Peaches hugged me with the love of a sister and the strength of a WWF wrestler.

"Let me breathe, girl."

"Sorry, sister-twin," Peaches sniffled. "You know how I get."

Jimmy's niece asked, "What happened?"

Slowly, painfully, the story left my lips, as told to me, as seen by me, as experienced by me. By the end, not a sistah there had a dry eye.

His niece shook her head. "Is Uncle Jimmy going to die?"

Peaches held her hand. "None of that talk now. Jimmy'll be okay, you watch and see."

"Uncle Jimmy was surely off the deep end to murder somebody! How am I going to tell Grandma?"

"Just pray," Peaches said, hugging her. "That's all you can do."

We sat there for over an hour, huddled together, collectively sending up prayers, waiting for some word from the doctor. When the ER physician finally came into the emergency room, she explained that they'd done all they could and that Jimmy was stable. Now all anyone could do was just wait and see.

I struggled with my thoughts—rambling thoughts with no speed limit and no direction. Jimmy had been in cahoots with Guy Weaver? How did they meet? When did they get together to hatch this plot? Jimmy had buckled under the strain of their conspiracy and nearly killed himself. He couldn't answer these questions. Guy Weaver could, but only the police had access to him.

I, however, had access to the people who *knew him and who knew Jimmy*.

I ended up using a photo the *Chicago Sun-Times* ran of Guy Weaver and a picture of Jimmy that his niece happened to have in her wallet. I went to WJIV. I waited for my favorite cameraman, and then this sister went to work.

First stop: Jimmy's apartment building.

Outside the ball of graying clouds hovered just below the luke-warm winter sun. The light it shed seemed like a shroud against the dingy buildings on the street. Jimmy lived in a pocket of poverty on the Southeast Side near the lakefront; a pocket that's patched and worn like the insides of a pair of old trousers.

The land was valuable to those who owned it; once big-time, then forgotten, and now on the verge of being star-quality real estate again. But fame is slow, especially when it comes to street corners and rehabbing. And in this section where Jimmy and other African-Americans sat in wait with their heads hung low in a penniless stu-por, there seemed to be no mercy.

It was Thursday morning. The hopeful stood on the corners beneath clear, plastic enclosures protecting against the Chicago wind as they waited for the bus to work or to school. They almost looked like astronauts in capsules, except their expressions were somewhere between *ho-hum* and *trapped*.

I never thought about where Jimmy lived or how he lived. Trapped. That must be how he felt in these surroundings most days, yet his spirit was so lively; the music inside my man Jimmy must have been his floatation device.

Jimmy's building was a weather-beaten gray stone three stories high, double-sided. On the front step sat an African-American man about sixty years old. He wore a dark blue sailor pea coat, double-breasted, paint-stained jeans, and construction boots. His hair was completely white and he kept looking up and down the street until he spotted Zeke and me walking toward him.

"Georgia Barnett, Channel 8 News," I said.

I extended my hand.

"Stan Reynolds." He shook my hand. "I've been on TV so much this week, I oughtah get an agent."

"I hear you, man." Zeke smiled and began setting up the shot from behind me. "I'm rolling."

"Have you lived here long?" I asked Stan.

"Yep, my cousin owns the building. I'm the janitor. Fix this and that. Let folks in when they lock themselves out—*for a fee.* Waiting to let a deliveryman in now, tenant getting a new sofa bed. *But I'm a TV star when something jumps off around here!*"

We all laughed.

"So, of course, you know Jimmy, and you know what's going on."

"Yeah, sure, I'm hip. Jimmy is a nice guy. Don't believe he murdered nobody. We play dominoes all the time. He's cool. He gets behind on his rent, but catches up when he can. Plays the hell out of a get-tar."

I pulled out a photo of Guy Weaver. "You've probably seen Guy Weaver on the news. This is a better picture of him. Did you ever see him with Jimmy?"

Stan looked at it. Turned his head left. Frowned. Turned his head right. Frowned. "Naw. I never saw him with Jimmy. And I keep a good lookout. I'm Security too."

"When you guys played dominoes together, did Jimmy ever mention Guy Weaver?"

He thought, then shook his head. "Naw."

"Okay," I said. "Thanks anyway. Listen, we're gonna run inside for a few minutes—knock on a few doors, talk to some of the other tenants."

"Go ahead."

Zeke and I went from door to door. We got a variety of responses:

"Don't know him."

"No. Hell no. And get on 'way from here."

"Yeah, I've seen him. That's one of them TV people on 'Survivor,' isn't it?"

Gimme a break.

Our next stop was down the block, the corner grocery store. The front door was buckled wood, peeling green paint falling at your feet when you opened it. Inside, the floor wasn't even tiled; it was concrete. There were about six aisles. You could stand at the front door and look down all of them and practically tell if they had what you wanted.

Behind the counter, a big-boned woman sat on a stool. She had thick hair, bushy around her ears, a wide face, a charcoal mole on her left cheek, clothes made of polyester, nutmeg and creme-colored, swirled around her torso, up nearly to her chin.

"Help you?" she said and the words crackled with the weight of her accent. She smiled warmly, pointing at the camera, "TV? TV?"

"Relax, my friend," Zeke cooed from behind the viewfinder.

"Can you tell me if you've seen this man around here before?"

She looked at Guy's picture and immediately shook her head no. I showed her Jimmy's picture. "He might have been with this man, Jimmy Flamingo—"

"Yes, my friend. Nice man, never causes trouble."

"So you haven't seen the two men around together?"

She shook her head no again.

And so it went. This is the foot soldier part of TV news—it kicks the stew out of the glamour stuff. A reporter has to walk up and down the street, stopping whomever to ask them whatever. And the response? Give me Jesus! It can be some of everything—getting barked at by snarly dogs or talked to death by some lonely person shortchanged in the good-sense department.

Like Gladys Knight and the Pips used to sing: "On and on. Gotta keep moving. On and on." Looking for a clue: a little something-

something to add to your story. This whole Fab Weaver murder story was no piece of sweet potato pie, I'm here to tell you.

No one had ever seen Jimmy with Guy Weaver. I even went to his hole-in-the-wall gambling joint—had to leave Zeke outside, those old school players weren't about to let me put them on video front and center. None of Jimmy's ace boon-coons had seen him with Guy Weaver or even heard Jimmy mention his name.

Jimmy is a talented musician, a genius in that respect, but a plotter? *Jimmy couldn't keep a plan together with staples and glue!*

Jimmy's never been a leader—could solo the hell out of a performance but failed with every band he tried to put together according to Peaches and the other folks I talked with.

So I stopped stalking the trail of the follower and began tracking the path of the probable leader.

Chapter Seventeen

NEXT STOP: GUY WEAVER'S NEIGHBORHOOD.

As Zeke put the pedal to the metal in our Channel 8 News truck
we took the swerves and curves of North Lake Shore Drive with
abandon and urgency.

The wind hiked up Lake Michigan's blue skirt, showing off the
frothy white slip underneath before it shyly slid back into place.

The drive separates the lake from the bustling high-rises with
their aerial views and rents. Big-boned trees looked even more
muscular without their leaves as they lined the boulevards. Cars
snuggled bumper to bumper like teenagers on a love seat. Guy lived
in a well-desired yet overcrowded area with scarcely any parking
space.

And you know Zeke. Sometimes he can act like *he don't have a bit
of sense.* Zeke eyeballed what should have been room for two legal
spots between a fire hydrant and a No Parking sign. A small Fiat was
there, hogging the extra space.

"Hey, remember that dance called the bump?" Zeke threw the
truck in reverse.

Bing!

"Doing the bump." He laughed. "Put your backside into it!"

Bing-bing!

"You ain't right." I got out and looked. We were in. "Zeke, you know you ain't right."

"I ain't right," he grinned, "but I know how to roll."

We walked into Guy Weaver's building, teal-tinted glass from floor to ceiling, waterfall cascading in the corner next to an expensive set of leather seats.

The doorman was happy to see me, probably feeling his wallet getting twenty bucks heavier. He said that he'd never seen Jimmy with Guy Weaver, that Guy was a loner. That Guy never had any visitors except for his father, their lawyer, and a maid once. Said he didn't know how the man lived, never saw Guy come in the place with even a grocery bag. That his father bought him food, clothes, even the cheap furniture they had moved in a week or so ago. There was no lead here, I realized, so the news groove goes on.

I went to Guy Weaver's rehab center.

The receptionist remembered me from my first visit. She politely told me that Mrs. Hopson was in a meeting with the parents of one of the patients. She would be available shortly. I told her not to worry about bothering her just yet—I wanted to ask some of the staff people if they'd seen Guy Weaver with Jimmy. I showed the receptionist the photo first. She said no.

Next. Saw two other counselors; they said no. Asked the receptionist to page the janitor; she did. And he recognized Jimmy from the news reports but not from hanging around the center with Guy Weaver. No one had seen them together here either. I thought, *What is the linchpin between these two men?*

Then Mrs. Hopson came out of a rear conference room. She smiled at me. And baby, it was a phony-baloney one. She rushed those parents right out the door as quickly as she could. Then Mrs. Hopson turned and looked at me again like I was at the top of her shit list.

Her jaws were tight as the skirt on a ten-dollar whore. Her face was pale too. I could see her shoulders shift back with each labored breath. Even Zeke noticed.

"The welcome wagon's got a busted wheel!"

I threw a soft elbow to his ribs. "Hush up, you!" Then, with the home training I was given, I said, "Hi, Jean. How's every—"

"Address me as Mrs. Hopson, please."

"Oh, sorry." *Now that's foul. What's got her panties in a bunch?* "Is something wrong?"

"Yes. And I plan on telling you about it. *Off the record.*"

I was a bit distracted. Over Mrs. Hopson's shoulder, I could see right through a door into a fairly large classroom. A group of teenagers was meeting. They sat in a semicircle. Must have been a dozen or so of them. A young woman, in her twenties, and a young man, also in his twenties, seemed to be running the class.

"Oh, I see that class in there caught your eye?" Mrs. Hopson said rather curtly. "That's for recovering teenage addicts. They live at a halfway house at night. During the day, we have GED classes here."

"Great. Sounds like a good program."

"It is. That's Guy Weaver's class."

Guy taught a class?

"Yes," she said, reading my mind. "He taught a class. For free. Literature. He even bought books for some of the more talented kids."

"How nice."

"Isn't it," Mrs. Hopson said, putting her hands on her hips. "Not at all like the man you described in your television report."

"Umph!" Zeke grunted.

"Mrs. Hopson, I reported the facts as I had them. I gave you an opportunity to talk about Guy, remember? You declined."

"I'm not supposed to talk about the personal lives of patients past or present. You said you wanted to be fair and you weren't."

"I went with what I had," I said, throwing my hands up then letting them flop back down to my sides. "Just like you work with what you have here. I put every fact I had into that piece. You were stand-ing right here when your janitor said that Guy Weaver was not at the center all night. He had opportunity."

"That doesn't mean he's guilty. My gut tells me two things, Ms. Barnett. Guy didn't do this. And two, you painted a lopsided picture of him. Why? I'm not sure—"

"I don't slant my stories—"

"Maybe you didn't work as hard to see the other side of Guy? Maybe that's what happened?"

I got a bitter taste in my mouth. Had I been in such a hurry to find anything to make Guy look bad, just because I wanted so badly to help Jimmy? Even now, with the evidence mounting against him and Jimmy both, had my coverage been biased?

"I'd be more than happy to let you tell everyone what you know about Guy as a person, the positive side."

"I cannot."

I huffed, getting frustrated. And man, when I get frustrated, my gut churns like it's making butter. What did she want from me? Ste-vie Wonder could see she wanted something. But what?

"I really can't. Some of the students here can, if they want. And there's a tape."

"A tape?"

"Yes, you can get it from the receptionist. Ask her for a copy of the video we give to parents who put their teens in our educational program."

"Thank you," I said. "And you can bet that I will use it. I'm not trying to railroad Guy. I'm trying to get to the truth. I take pride in what I do—just like you. If I've been unfair, then I'll make it right."

I'd gotten popped in the chops; sistah can't stand to get her chops popped either. I've worked hard to pay my dues, not to mention the way I bust a gut every news day.

After interviewing a couple of students, Zeke and I headed back to the station. Once there, we would take a look at the video and interviews we had shot. We'd also dub this VHS tape over to Beta so that it could be edited into my package.

We got back to WJIV and the newsroom was buzzing as usual. Two writers were hunched over their computer screens banging out copy for the first newscast of the afternoon. Clarice was sitting at the desk, a phone on each ear, staring at a map of the city, trying to jockey camera crews around.

I put in the tape from North Shore New Life Center. Was I surprised? Yes.

The video started out average enough, showing teenagers using drugs; it looked like file footage from some old documentary. The video was not slick, though the voice-over announcer had pipes like James Earl Jones, so it was an *easy-pleasy* listen.

Then it cut to exteriors of the center, to the classroom I saw. Guy Weaver was holding court, teaching the students about Tennyson. Guy's face was shiny with enthusiasm, his voice gutsy yet comforting. One student stood up and read a poem about loneliness, hope, and recovering with courage. Guy reached out and took her hand, drew her into him, and gave her a hug with several gentle pats on the back. It was a beautiful hug. I stopped the video and looked closely. Several of the other students were clearly moved to tears.

Is this the same man who dreamed about killing his own father? I was surprised at how strong this part of Guy's personality was. He seemed warm. Caring. Gentle.

There are surely two sides to everyone, yet usually the degree of difference is slight and each side is interwoven like the threads of a spider's web. My man Guy's sides clashed as much as a striped shirt and checkered pants.

I knew how I was going to write my afternoon piece on this story. The lead-in, which the anchor reads, would give the hard-news angle; that's the fact that Jimmy overdosed. It would also include his condition coupled with a gun being found and checked to see if it was the murder weapon. Bang had refused to talk to anyone on camera about the ordeal. I understood.

So the body of my piece would be about Guy Weaver and the side he showed at the center. I was trying to put the pieces together. I'd found no link between Guy and Jimmy; and I'd seen a side of Guy that showed extreme compassion. A clean Guy. I owed it to the viewing public to show that side.

I wrote my piece, put it together with the help of an editor and a staff writer. Then I sat at my desk and watched my story air, live.

(NATURAL SOUND—CENTER VIDEO)

"You're young. Stay drug-free. Don't make the same mistakes I have."

MY VOICE TRACK COMES UP FULL SOUND BENEATH THE VIDEO THAT I'D GOTTEN FROM MRS. HOPSON.

"This is Guy Weaver as you've never seen him before. He's making an emotional plea to a group of teenagers at the drug rehab center. This video is handed out to parents who want to help their troubled teens get drug-free. That goal has been reached for some of the teens, and they say it's because of Guy Weaver."

(SOUND BITE—STUDENT)

"Because Guy has had a drug problem, he can understand where we're coming from."

"Guy Weaver is a recovering addict, struggling with a cocaine problem. While at this drug rehab center, he began volunteering to teach an English class that would help the troubled teens get their high school diplomas."

(NATURAL SOUND OF KID READING POEM)

My voice track comes up under the video of Guy hugging the student.

"Guy not only taught students about poetry, he taught them about caring. Here, he and his class embrace a student who many people had given up on. But not Guy. Not the class."

(STUDENT SOUND BITE)

"If it wasn't for this center, all the people here, I'd probably be dead somewhere. Now I've got a chance."

"Guy Weaver is himself hoping for a chance, a chance to convince police that he is not a killer. Tonight Guy is behind bars as police investigate leads that he and bluesman Jimmy Flamingo may have killed Guy's father, record producer Fab Weaver."

(SOUND BITES OF PEOPLE SAYING THEY HAVEN'T SEEN THE TWO MEN TOGETHER)

"No, I haven't seen them around here. No. No."

My track continues under b-roll of both neighborhoods where we showed pictures of Guy and Jimmy.

"From Jimmy Flamingo's neighborhood on the South Side to Guy Weaver's neighborhood on the North Shore, no one

has ever seen these two men together. Guy's supporters say
they are behind him one hundred percent."

(SOUND BITE—STUDENT)

"We believe Guy and we're praying for him."

"Tonight we don't know for sure whether or not Guy
Weaver is capable of murder. But what we do know for sure
is that he has been a teacher—a man who has extended help
to others. Now that same sense of compassion is being
extended to him by those at the rehab center. Georgia Barnett, Channel 8 News."

I GOT SOME KUDOS ON MY PIECE AND FELT REAL COOL ABOUT
it. I'd been working like a d-o-g and was glad folks were giving me
my props. In this little space of downtime I started to realize how
tired and hungry I was. I had begun the short walk to the corner deli
to pick up my order when my pager fired up.

It was Doug, so I whipped out my cell phone and gave him a buzz.
"Hey, what's up?"

"Look, Georgia, we got a break in the case."

"What?"

"I think we found the car."

"Where?"

"I'm headed over to a garage where they've been fencing stolen
vehicles. Got a call from a friend working the undercover operation.
They've been watching the spot for about two months. The bust went
down late this morning. Quite a few arrests were made. Some of the
boys found a box of crushed license plates. One of the plates was
BUG 313."

"That's the plate from the missing rent-a-car!"

"Yeah, we're getting the serial number from the rent-a-car company so we can go through some of the vehicles they've got. Some of the cars were stripped for parts, other cars were repainted and sold down South."

"Neat little setup they had there, huh?"

"That's for sure. I know for a fact that the undercover boys have tipped off some of the other TV stations. They want to get the positive pub for busting the theft ring. I asked my buddy to keep it on the down low about the plate, just in case the car isn't there. But with the link to the Fab Weaver murder case, you better get a camera and hightail it down here pronto."

Doug gave me the address. "Thanks, baby. Say, what about Guy? What's he saying?"

"Nothing so far except that he's innocent. That Jimmy's lying. Horace Hightower hired him a criminal attorney. His attorney is muzzling him now. Tellin' him to keep quiet."

"You know, I've been working their connection all afternoon and can't find one person who saw them together."

"We're checking their phone records for the last couple of weeks, to see if they've made any calls to one another. Ballistics is still working on the gun. How's Jimmy?"

"Still in a coma. I left Peaches and his niece at the hospital. How's Bang?"

"Took his statement and sent the brother home. It's traumatic having to turn in your friend after he's overdosed on your bathroom floor."

"Yeah, it's been a rough ride for everybody. Look, I'll see you at the crime scene. Thanks again, Doug, I owe you."

"Anything for you, girl."

I told Zeke about this latest break in the story. He just shook his head and looked up at the sky. "Miss Barnett, you got a hot one, huh?"

"Zeke, the drama never stops."

"Let's hit it then!"

The garage where the theft ring operated was about twenty minutes away from WJIV. By the time we got there, two cameramen from other television stations were already in place shooting b-roll of the stripped cars. A long table was set up to display four handguns, theft tools, and cash that the police had managed to confiscate.

I saw Doug looking at a black car, a Cavalier, in the rear of the garage. Zeke and I made our way over. Doug said, "This is the bad boy we want. They painted it but hadn't gotten around to stripping the vehicle identification number."

An evidence tech had the rear door open, dusting the handle for prints. Zeke was busy filming it. Doug said to me, "Get a shot of the backseat. There's a bullet hole on the passenger side."

Zeke leaned over the back of the evidence tech and zoomed in on the hole.

"We've got the gun. The car. Bang's statement about what Jimmy said. Guy Weaver's looking at a first-degree murder charge."

I had a hell of a story on my hands. The developments were coming fast and furious. Jimmy's revelation and drug overdose. The recovery of the murder weapon and the car. Guy Weaver soon to be charged.

The cop shop looked like a zoo. Every media outlet was camped out waiting to get a shot of Guy Weaver being transferred to court for arraignment. His lawyer had told him to button his lip, and he had, not saying any more since being brought in.

When Guy Weaver emerged from a rear door, cuffed and crumpled, sweating like he was *jonesin'* for a hit, looking whupped as hell, the crowd of television reporters pushed and shouted questions the way spectators in the Roman arena called for blood.

Guy, frazzled and fatigued, paused in the middle of his walk and yelled, "I didn't do it. Believe me."

He jerked his cuffed hands. "Why would I kill him. What for?"

One of my colleagues yelled, "To get his money!"

"That's ridiculous. My father wasn't leaving me a dime."

What? Fab Weaver had disinherited his son? So the strongest motive of wealth was gone? Was it pure hatred then?

By now the police escort was pissed off plenty—he grabbed Guy by the shoulder and steered him forward to a waiting paddy wagon.

Guy was charged with murder. Jimmy was still in a coma. Ballistics came back with confirmation that the .22 was indeed the murder weapon and Jimmy's prints were on it.

I ended my day after filing the latest story for the ten. I wasn't live at the cop shop but had what's called a set tag. Basically they go to you sitting alongside the anchors. At that point there are some questions and answers between the three of you.

Afterward I went straight home. I crawled into that bed like a caterpillar crawls into a hole. I slept clear through until the phone rang at 6:30 A.M. I had the Friday-morning blahs when I whined into the receiver, *"Whaaaaaat?"*

"Georgia, it's me, baby."

"Honey, I'm hurting." I yawned. "Give me another hour."

"It's Friday and what are we supposed to do on Friday mornings?"

"Aww, Doug no. *Please*, baby, no exercise."

"Yep, once a week. We're supposed to meet at the health club for a real workout. C'mon, we've been awful trifling lately. Be a great way to burn off some anxiety."

"All right, slide through in an hour."

"Forty-five minutes." *Click!*

I hate working out with Doug; he can do all the machines. He's so smooth and tight. I'm kindah slim but I've got *lumps in my pumps* for days. Mostly like around them there hips and thighs; they start getting *jiggie* with it as soon as I hit the StairMaster. But I had promised Doug. And who knows? Maybe it would be good to get my workout on.

We started out slow. The StairMaster felt foreign against the bottom of my feet. Hadn't been exercising like I knew I should. I huffed and puffed worse than an asthma patient. I wanted to call time-out, call my mama, dial 911 on my cell after one single sorry mile.

"It's hurting, huh, baby?" Doug said from the treadmill next to me.

I huffed out my answer. "Yes, ah mercy!"

Doug laughed, "Pit-E-ful!"

I leaned over and smashed my fingers against his speed button. "Show me the money, big mouth!"

Doug instantly became a combination of the comic/action duo Jackie Chan and Chris Tucker. His arms were spanking the air wildly as he kept speed, fighting for balance, all the while with an irresistible grin, wide eyes, and a playful tongue. *"Whoa-whoa-ahh-hhhh, whoop-whoop!"*

I slammed my palm down on the stop button and Doug's arms jerked back in the air as he went in reverse, flying off the back of the machine. He landed in the arms of a bucktoothed Monica Lewinsky lookalike. She began squeezing him tight.

Baby, I got off that StairMaster and marched over to Miss Thing like I was still working out on *mountainous incline.*

"Look what I caught!" she said, batting her eyes.

"Catch a cold. This man is for sisters only!"

She rolled her eyes and sashayed away. I couldn't help chuckling to myself.

Doug was amused too, digging on how I had made a quick move to claim him as my property.

"C'mon, let's hit the sauna; that'll take some of the friskiness out of you."

Doug circled his arm around my shoulders. I circled my arm around his waist. We walked toward the sauna room. The sweat felt good cascading down my back. "Doug?"

"Hmmmm..."

"What'll happen to Jimmy, after he gets well?"

"Be charged. Held without bond."

"This story is bugging me. Hotheaded as both Jimmy and Guy Weaver can get, I'm not feeling it in my bones that they did it. I mean, why would Jimmy hook up with Guy Weaver? I don't see a connection. I checked their main hangouts—the neighborhoods. Couldn't find a connection. You checked their phones, they didn't call each other..."

Doug stopped walking. "Shit! That's my pager." He looked at it. "One of the boys helping on this case."

"Here, use my cell," I offered, fishing it out of my waist pouch. I watched anxiously as Doug made the call. His eyes darted around. I could tell he was thinking.

"What?" he said. "That is odd. Are you sure about the time? Good, okay. I'll check it out. Thanks."

"What is it, Doug?"

"Did you use the phone the day you went to Fab Weaver's house? The day after the body was found."

"No, I didn't use the phone."

"We checked his phone records. Trying to see who he saw and spoke to last. You know, see if there's a pattern of callers."

"I'm with you."

"Well, there was a call listed to Horace Hightower."

"So, that's his attorney."

"So, the time was odd. It was the day after the body was recovered from the lake. Fab Weaver was already dead. At the time the call was made, only a small group of people had access to the phone."

"You didn't make the call," I reasoned out loud. "I didn't make the call. And I'm damn sure Zeke didn't."

"Right, Georgia. That leaves one other person. Why would she be calling Fab Weaver's attorney?"

"Let's ask her."

Chapter Eighteen

ANGELINA ROSSENI LIVED IN A RUN-DOWN APARTMENT over a grocery store and mechanic's shop on the West Side. A soft drizzly rain was beginning to fall as we parked.

Doug and I sprinted up the stairs. We did not ring her doorbell. We wanted to bum-rush Angelina before she could get her thoughts or her lies together. Doug banged long and hard on the door. After about five minutes I could hear slow, dragging footsteps coming toward the front of the apartment.

The dead bolt slid back and the door was slowly cracked open. The only safety now was a link chain that sagged like a kid's jump rope just above the deep furrows in Angelina's surprised brow. "Yeah?"

Doug flashed his badge. "Remember me? Detective Eckart. Sorry to bother you at home. I'd like to ask you a couple of more questions regarding the murder of Fab Weaver."

Angelina closed her robe, looked very nervous, her eyes darting around. "Well, I'm not decent, Detective . . ."

Her voice took on a coarse register. Girlfriend was trying to loud-talk the brother.

". . . is it normal for you guys to come to someone's house this time of morning?"

"It'll only take a minute, Ms. Rosseni, I assure you."

"Well, I'm not accustomed to letting men I don't know into my apartment, even if they are on the police force. I'm just not comfortable with it."

I stepped into view. "I'm here too."

Angelina swallowed, "Oh."

"My presence put you at ease before, remember? When you were being questioned at Mr. Weaver's house? Maybe it will again now."

"Either that," Doug said, "or I can wait for you to dress and you can come down to the station—that's the long, tedious way."

"Hang on," Angelina said, closing the door, sliding the chain off, then opening the door all the way, allowing us in.

Expensive leather furniture filled the scant space of the one-bedroom apartment. There was a couch the color of whipped cream; a matching love seat and ottoman. The set was anchored by an oak cocktail table with two end tables. Lush drapes, cream with speckled roses around the border, framed her windows. The drapes were generously cut, dragging the floor.

Girlfriend had expensive taste and the cash to pull it off. Where'd a house cleaner get this kind of first national cash? Something was up. Felt it in my bones, child. I exchanged glances with Doug. He knew it too. I said, "Nice furniture, Angelina."

"Uhm, thanks. I got a good deal on it."

Angelina and Doug sat down on the couch. I sat on the love seat. I tried to chat her up, put her at ease while Doug pulled out his interview pad and pen. "My sister Peaches loves leather furniture. She just bought some for the little office space she has above her club, the Blues Box. Paid a hand and a foot for it too."

"Too bad."

"All right, Angelina," Doug said, ready to start. "I just have a few questions, then we'll be out of your way."

"Okay."

"Now, Tuesday morning you were working at the victim's house."

"Right," Angelina answered. She seemed edgy, her lips pulled in a taut line.

"Was there anyone else who came in that morning?"

"No," she said without having to so much as think about it.

"So until Georgia Barnett and her cameraman came, you were alone in the house working as usual?"

"Yes."

"How long had you worked for Fab Weaver?"

"A little over a year."

"And how long have you known his attorney, Horace Hightower?"

She only clutched her clothing tighter, like she felt exposed somehow. But every inch of Angelina Rosseni was covered.

"I don't know him really. He signs my paychecks. I've never actually met him."

That's what Angelina told me. She didn't know him. Never met him. And didn't know his phone number.

"Then why did you call him Tuesday morning when you were interviewed by Ms. Barnett?" Doug asked.

"What are you talking about?" Angelina said, picking at a strand of hair hanging flat against her neck.

"We checked the phone records at the victim's house. There was a call made from the phone in the study that morning. A small group of people had access. You. The cameraman. Georgia. Me. We didn't make the call and the call was to Horace Hightower's home."

"You lied. Why?" I asked.

"I don't know what you're talking about. And I really don't feel like answering any more questions. I'm tired."

"Well," Doug said, "you are a witness in a murder case. I think I'll officially ask you to come down to the station so that we can go over your entire testimony once more."

"Is that necessary, detective?"

"You just made it necessary."

"So just like that, huh? You're just gonna drag me out of here half-naked?"

"I'll wait until you're dressed."

Like lightning streaking across the sky, anger erupted in Angelina's eyes. She didn't move a toe. "This is so unnecessary."

Doug looked from Angelina to the bedroom door and back again.

"All right," she said, heading toward the bedroom. "I'll be back in a minute."

I shrugged at Doug.

He mouthed the word, "Pressure."

Then Doug whispered to me, "Don't know what Angelina's hiding but she's hiding something."

"Horace Hightower is the common denominator, Doug. He's got some connection to Angelina . . ."

Doug picked up the list of connections. ". . . he represented the victim and his son Guy. And Hightower was fighting Jimmy's efforts to bring a lawsuit."

"He bears another talking-to," I said to Doug, still unsure of how all these pieces would jell.

Doug nodded, then called, "Angelina, hurry up."

There was no answer.

"Angelina?" Doug ran to the bedroom door and used his shoulder like a key. The wood howled as he lurched against it, giving up the lock *easy-pleasy.* I was right on Doug's heels.

The weather was changing. A high wind made the room ice cold. Next to the fire escape was an open window. The lush drapes flapped in and out, telling the story of Angelina's flight like a gossiping tongue.

What made her run? Angelina had thrown on her clothes and bolted out of the window. Why? Angelina was the one who described Jimmy as the man who threatened to kill Fab Weaver. She was the one who identified him, putting him at the house the day before the murder.

There were two dresser drawers open in the room with the unkempt bed and the small lamp with the lace shade. One of the dressers had a bunch of papers in it.

Doug was rambling through it. A bank deposit slip caught my eye, only because it had a lot of zeros. For the love of money! Angelina had some mean, mean green. "Look at this." I showed Doug. "Twenty-five thousand in her checking account. Says there's a hold on it."

He took the statement. "That deposit was made yesterday, takes time to clear."

Angelina had an apartment full of expensive furniture and had recently deposited $25,000. She had a connection to Horace Hightower, a rich attorney. Called him when her boss turned up murdered. Helped to finger Jimmy for the crime.

Doug was hot, mad that Angelina had put the scurry on us. He alerted all squads in the area. They would be on the lookout for her in every crack and crevice. The check Angelina deposited—the $25,000—hadn't cleared yet. Did she have enough to get far? Or how far could she get on what she had?

Doug sent two detectives to pick up Horace Hightower. He wanted to talk to him extensively he said—at the station.

I had to make it to bond court. Guy Weaver was going before a judge.

Bond is a funny thing. Sometimes a judge will grant it and sometimes he won't. Sometimes bond is set high. Sometimes it's set low. Usually there are parameters so that the process is consistent and fair. But when the state's attorney's office begins to argue against someone who is a flight risk or if the crime is particularly heinous, bond can go up. You need 10 percent, which is bail.

Guy Weaver's bond was set at half a million dollars. He needed $50,000 to bail himself out.

I sent him a note as he sat in bond court. It simply said, "Can we talk? We might be able to help each other."

When I sent the note I wasn't sure that Guy would get out immediately. But his criminal attorney arranged for him to use his father's property to make bond. Guy was bailed and walking the media gauntlet to his car. Everyone was pushing and shoving, asking questions, running after the car, trying to get in position to get the best shot.

I got out of Zeke's way. Let him run to get the money shot, pushing and shoving with the rest, staying in place and in focus as the car pulled off. Guy waved to the camera from the comfort of the heated Lincoln Town Car. Then he gave them the finger as the driver pulled off.

I watched from a distance. Normally I would be in the thick of it like the other reporters and cameramen. But all we needed was the shot itself, not the grunts of "no comment" from Guy Weaver's *slick rick* criminal attorney.

I had something better. A court officer gave me an envelope with my name on it. I opened it. It was Guy Weaver agreeing to sit down with me and talk. No cameras though. No criminal attorney. The sit-down would be at his apartment two hours from now.

When I arrived, Guy Weaver was still in a wrecked state. He had a scruffy beard, bags under his eyes from lack of sleep; he had lost weight and didn't need to lose nary a pound. County jail ain't no beauty shop, kiddo.

"I saw the story you did about me. It was very nice." Guy's voice was stronger, his gaze steady, unlike before when I had interviewed him. "You believe I'm innocent now, don't you?"

"Guy, in my job I try not to guess one way or the other. I just forge ahead and make an effort to dig out the truth."

"The truth is I didn't kill him, even though my father made my life hell growing up. I do admit to trying to return the favor by running wild—but that's it."

"Guy, every bully I ever knew loved to see you beat yourself up with fear first. Made their job easier. You hurt yourself more than you did him."

Guy pulled out a package of cigarettes and lit one. "You're probably right. Smoke?"

"No, thanks. How well do you know Jimmy Flamingo?"

"I don't. My lawyer told me the police think he and I plotted together to kill my father. I don't know the man aside from his old records. I'm innocent and that's the truth. I want you to believe me and I want you to help me."

"Then you have to answer any questions I have—truthfully, no b.s."

"Fine."

"Good. Now there is someone else I've been wondering about. What do you know about your father's attorney, Horace Hightower?"

"He's handled my father's business ever since I can remember." Guy twisted his mouth to the left and blew a swirl of gray smoke into the air. "They go way back. They met in some hole-in-the-wall gym. My father was a boxer for a while, semipro. Hightower worked at the gym while finishing up law school."

"So whose idea was it to start the record company?"

"My father's. He got busted up pretty bad after a fight and spent a lot of time at home in bed. Didn't have a TV so he listened to the radio all day—said he developed an ear for what was a hit and what wasn't."

"Where'd he get the money to start the company?"

"Hightower introduced him to a rich law school friend of his, that's where. Then later my father paid the guy back with interest. He asked Hightower to help him with the legal stuff when the gold records started rolling in."

"So they both did pretty well, huh?"

"Yeah, but it was my father's baby. He's the one who made the killing. Hightower still worked for my father. He's tight as hell with my old man's money—when it comes to me, not himself."

"What do you mean by that?"

"I mean he'd go on trips with other women, leave his wife at home. Expense it sometimes to my father's account until my father made him cut that crap out."

"Your father told you this?"

"In a rare moment of communication. Dad had stopped by to see the five thousand dollars' worth of furniture that he told Hightower to buy and send over to me."

Couldn't help but look around at the Kmart specials decorating the room.

"Yeah." Guy laughed, squashing the butt in a metal ashtray. "That's what I did. Just looked at this junk. Couldn't have paid more than a grand, if that. My father flipped out! Said that Mr. Hightower was spending too much of his money on *what he wanted.* Dad called him on the phone and chewed him out."

"So what happened next?"

"My father wanted to send this lovely ensemble back. But just to screw with the old man, I told him, no. Told him I liked it. It reminded me of him—cheap."

"That went over big."

"Very," Guy said, touching his jaw. "Got me a rap in the mouth. But hey, I'm used to that. Now what they couldah done was keep sending that cleaning lady over here to spruce up the place instead of just when this cheap-ass furniture was being delivered."

"Cleaning lady?"

"Yeah . . . what's her name, Ange . . ."

"Angelina Rosseni?"

"Yeah, the one in that story you did about my father. She said what a nice guy he was. *Give me a break.*"

"Angelina Rosseni cleaned your apartment? When?"

"The day before they were to deliver the new furniture, about two weeks ago. Hair was a different color then, but same girl, I recognized her."

"Guy, did she have access to the entire apartment?"

"Yeah, she cleaned from top to bottom. I left. Came back. Place was spotless."

"Now think. Did you have your credit card before she came to clean?"

"Yeah, I think so."

"How about afterward?"

"No." Guy scratched his chin. "Can't say that I can remember using it or seeing it afterward. Didn't have a reason to. You think she stole it?"

"Yeah, I do. She and Horace Hightower are hooked up together some kind of a way. The first person she called after finding out that your father was murdered was him—yet she denied ever meeting him before."

"Son of a bitch."

"Now, Guy, something you said before really bugged me."

"What?"

"When you were being arraigned, a reporter threw out the theory that you killed your father for his money. You said you weren't going to get a dime."

Guy ran his hands through his hair. "My father . . . he and I always went at it. His father abandoned him—never took care of him. So he had this thing about providing for his children. Dad told me that I would always be given the basics, but I'd never live the high life, not off his sweat."

"Well, who was going to get the money?"

"Mr. Hightower would control the money. Make sure half stayed in trust to be parceled out to me—go to my children if I had any—the other half would go to him."

"Hightower?"

"Yeah, if they weren't so damn macho I'd swear they were lovers. They were, sort of. They loved the ruthless way they ran that record business. They loved the fear they put into people. My father used to do it with his fists. Mr. Hightower does it with that high-powered law firm of his."

"Do you have a copy of the will? The one that shows that Horace Hightower would collect millions after your father's death?"

"No." Guy shrugged. "My father kept a copy in his office. Mr. Hightower has the other in his office. You think he has something to do with all this?"

"I think he's mixed up in this some kind of a way. Hightower had too much to gain and his mark is showing up in all the wrong places."

"Well, I know he couldn't stand me. Tried to hide it, but I could tell. But what about that musician guy?"

"Jimmy Flamingo?"

"Why'd he say that he knew me? I don't know him from Adam."

I shrugged. "I don't know. That's the kicker. I just don't know."

After I left Guy, I got in the news truck with Zeke.

"How'd it go?" he said.

"Good. Hightower is looking like the honcho here. I think he could be setting Guy up. He's connected with Angelina, who had access to Guy's apartment and the credit card that was stolen and used to rent the car for the night of the murder. Hightower also stood to collect millions of dollars when Fab Weaver died."

Zeke whistled through his teeth. "Dirty dog. Wouldn't sell him a cow that didn't give no milk!"

"What?" I said. Zeke had a bunch of old Alabama sayings that he'd pull out every blue moon and chuck at ya. But goodness, half the doggone time you didn't know what the heck they meant.

"See . . ."

"*Don't go there.* Drive."

"Where to?"

"To WJIV first. Then we'll go to Horace Hightower's office. We've got some sneakin' to do."

Chapter Nineteen

SOME FOLKS CALL IT COMMANDO JOURNALISM. SOME PEOPLE call it undercover surveillance. Sister-girl me calls it as I see it: a sneak peek is a *sneak peek.*

Zeke parked the news truck in a construction zone downtown, about two blocks away from Hightower's law office. We had to stop at the station first so I could change clothes and lose my fashion fair face. I needed to look like a young mailroom clerk.

Most reporters keep some casual clothes at work; never know where you'll be sent or when. I put on a pair of jeans, sneakers, and a sweat shirt. Put on a Chicago Bulls cap for good measure, hung it low to hide some of my reporter mug too.

I planned to get into Hightower's office, find that will, make a copy, and get the heck out of there. As long as I did not leave the property with the will, I was still on solid journalistic ground.

Doug was still questioning Hightower at the cop shop. I knew he was going to keep boyfriend awhile—I was hoping for the rest of the afternoon. But I couldn't be certain and I couldn't be caught.

"Welp!" Zeke said giving me the once-over. "You look like a regular old somebody. Now how you gonna get past that chick at the desk?"

"Oh shoot, let me think. What's her name? Betty?"

"Right, old Geritol on a stick."

"Ooooh, Zeke. You'll be a senior too one day."

"I'm planning on it. I just don't plan on being crotchety, know what I'm saying?"

"I hear you."

"Good. So hear this too. Don't get caught and land us both in the slammer."

"I have no intention of getting snagged, baby. Watch a sister work. Now, don't forget, Zeke. You meet me in Kinko's in thirty minutes."

"Got it. Let's do it."

My first stop was in the lobby of the building. There were three stores. A drugstore. A florist shop. And a Kinko's copy center. I went into Kinko's and bought three packs of five-hundred-count printer paper. Then I grabbed three FedEx packs, tore them open, took out the paper, and stuffed them inside.

I took two FedEx forms and filled them out. I made up some name like Winkin', Blinkin, & Nod, in New York, and checked the overnight box. I made *the receiver* Horace Hightower. I made up a fake name for the sender and laughed.

The third FedEx envelope I made *the sender* Horace Hightower. Getting past the guard at the front lobby desk was easy. I simply waited until he had a crowd at his station. At that point I started a brisk walk, making a jagged line to the stairs. I walked up to the second floor, came out, and went to the elevator. Hightower's office was on the tenth floor. I pulled my hat down over my eyes, held the FedEx packages up to my chest, partially covering the lower third of my face.

Betty was there, holding her ground, answering the phone. There was a man carrying a briefcase standing in front of her, fighting for her attention. I walked right over to the door, like I'd seen the woman do the day Zeke and I were there to interview Hightower. "Mail!" I called out like I sho nuff belonged.

Betty glanced over at me, hesitated. I said quickly, "I'm new. Man, these FedEx packages are heavy!" Betty simply nodded and hit the button.

The heavy glass doors seemed to take forever to open. The inside of my throat was scorched from my constant swallowing. I walked inside. It was very quiet, just a couple of people milling around. I walked as slowly as possible, as confidently as possible.

A dull knocking against the wall of my chest reminded me that I hate sneaking. Only if I have to, do I get on the down low like this. But in television news you do what you have to do.

I tried the door handle of Hightower's office. If that wasn't the loudest *click* I'd ever heard. I tiptoed inside and shut the door. Hightower had probably been stunned when the detectives showed up and asked him to take a ride with them. They surely must have caught boyfriend with his guard down. The desk was in disarray; he'd obviously been working awhile.

I went to the file cabinet, in the corner, by the window with its view of Chicago's astonishing lakefront. The drizzly rain had stopped, yet there was no sun, still clouds, but not so hazy as to mar the office view.

I began opening and closing the cumbersome drawers, flicking through the rainbow-colored tabs of the folders. I found an entire rack dedicated to Fab Weaver. I started from the back to the front, hoping to find the will.

Then I stopped.

I ran across a file that said Hit Time Records. It was a dense file. I pulled it out, my heart still taking pot shots at the insides of my chest. I flipped through financial statements. Big money. Millions. Fab Weaver had made a killin' back in the day. Then I came to a stapled set of pages, the top written in red, Potential Lawsuits. There were a bunch of names and occupations and a list of songs, etc.

I opened one of my FedEx packages, took out the blank paper, and slid this file in. I put the blank paper in the file so it wouldn't be empty. I kept looking, checking the clock. I'd been in here about ten minutes going on everlasting. I needed to get moving with a quickness.

Then I saw what I'd risked my neck for—the will. I opened another FedEx package, emptied out the paper, and put in the document. I put some of the blank paper in the empty file to pad it out, the rest I hurriedly mixed in with the work Hightower had left there.

I put the one dummy package I had left with the blank paper in it on top. Then I headed over to the door. I stopped and looked around the room. Despite my journalistic espionage it seemed as settled as it did when I first entered. Then I put my ear to the door and heard very little movement, and no voices. I cracked the door, again despising that loud click, then peeked out.

The coast looked clear, so I began speed-walking down the narrow hallway. Then I heard someone say, "Hey you!"

I can't be busted. I can't be busted.

"Say," a young man stopped me with a touch on my shoulder, "you must be new?"

I held the packages higher and nodded. "Yes."

"Well," the young man said, "it's tough enough being a new guy around here without the mail clerk forgetting to get my packages."

Then he looked at the top envelope I was carrying. It clearly had Hightower's name as the sender of the FedEx package. "Hightower's one of the big guys. I plan on being up there with him one day."

Then the young lawyer dropped a big envelope on top of my pile of packages. "I'm all the way at the end of the hall. Next time don't forget me."

"Yes, sir!" I said and got the heck out of there.

I made it downstairs to the Kinko's in the building. Zeke was waiting as planned by the self-copier. While I began poring over the documents I had bamboozled out of Hightower's law office, Zeke Xeroxed. We were blazing.

"Damn, Georgia," Zeke said, a pen doing a high-wire balancing act behind his ear, "we're moving so fast, I hardly know what I'm looking at."

"Just keep moving, I want to get these originals back to Hightower's office."

When we finished copying everything, I put all the originals in a new FedEx package and labeled it so that the *recipient* would be Hightower.

Zeke looked at the name I wrote down for the *sender,* reading out loud: "Christie Love? You crack me up, know that?"

I smiled at Zeke as I took that package *plus* the young lawyer's package and dropped them both off at the front desk. "These go upstairs. Mailroom made an error." I'd pulled it off. *Say-say, feeling good. Then next thing you know, I was feeling bad.*

It was about an hour and a half later and we were now about a block away from WJIV. I had Doug meet me at a little knickknack shop there. The owner was a friend of mine and allowed us to use her office for a little conference.

"You let Hightower go?" I shouted at Doug.

"Georgia, what could I hold him on?"

"Murder."

"His prints ain't on the gun."

"What about Angelina? What about that connection?"

"He had a good explanation for that," Doug said, relaxing on the corner couch in the tiny room.

"Like what?"

"Said he and Angelina were having an affair. Hightower says that he met her while interviewing people for the housecleaning job for Fab Weaver. The man says that he bought her nice things, they went on a couple of little trips, but that she started to get too possessive."

"And what does Hightower's wife say?"

"That's the twenty-five-thousand-dollar answer. Said Angelina threatened to spill the beans unless he paid her off, so he did."

"Why'd she call Hightower from the study then?"

"He claims that Angelina was upset about Fab Weaver's death and that she only wanted to be consoled. Apparently, Angelina's a loner and very much in love with Hightower. She naturally reached out to the person she cared for most, who could best advise and console her."

"That sounds like some doggone mess, Hightower would say."

"That is what he said. Damn near verbatim. I had to let him go, baby."

"You couldn't hold him a second longer?"

"Georgia, Hightower is an attorney. He knows the deal. He answered all the questions. The boy was extremely cool. And what am I gonna hold him on? Having an affair? You think the jails are overcrowded now? Make that a crime and we'll be herding 'em in two by two."

"What about the will? That's motivation for murder, isn't it? He's going to inherit millions!"

"Georgia, it ain't a crime to be a lucky motherfucker either. Hightower's partner is leaving him the piggy bank. Don't get me wrong, Georgia. I'm with you. I think he's in this up to his nostrils, okay? But I've got to get something concrete. I need something or somebody to put Hightower in this firmly. That, I'm sorry to say, I don't have."

"Well, maybe I can help you get it."

"How's that?"

"When I do my story this evening? I'll turn up the heat on Mr. Hightower. Maybe that will shake something loose—or somebody."

Chapter Twenty

THERE'S AN OLD R&B TUNE THAT SAYS, "SHAKE IT UP tonight!" But who needed that the way my week was going? I was beat, tired, weary; just downright fatigued when I finally got home.

Now, let me explain. My lack of energy had a muting effect, slithering through my limbs until I was limp as a rag. I fell face down on my body pillow and wrapped my legs around it, squeezing with all my might, wishing that it were a sponge that could absorb all my puzzlement and apprehension. When I sleep hard, baby, I sleep hard.

Shake it up tonight!

The phone started ringing and ringing. I couldn't pull myself out of that trance until I heard my sister Peaches talking on my answering machine.

"*Sister-twin!* Get up from there, girl. Right now."

She was begging, pleading. I thought, *Oh my God, Jimmy's gone.* I fumbled with the phone, yanking at the cord to free the receiver from its cradle.

"Hey-hey," I said sleepily. "I'm up."

"Georgia—"

"Jimmy's not—"

"Oh no! Don't even say it. Don't put that negative vibe out in the universe."

I exhaled, not even aware that I was holding my breath till I released it and my lungs felt like they were a couple of burning bushes. "Peaches, it's almost three o'clock in the morning. *Doggone* your time!"

"Don't matter, Georgia. Shake, rattle, and roll your skinny butt down here to the club."

"Please, twin, please!" Then I rolled over and balled myself up into a knot. *"Call me later!"*

"Look, we closed at two. Me and a couple of the boys from the band were locking up the joint. Then I had a visitor. Well, you're the one who's been shakin' the trees looking for some information to fall out. Well, it done fell out."

"Fell out how?"

"Hard and on top of my head! That's how."

"Who is it?" I groaned.

"They won't let me say. If I say, they walk, sister-twin."

"It's too early in the morning for drama, Peaches. If this is a joke I'm gonna be all over you like flies on a picnic lunch."

"Would I fool with you in the morning as *fun-kay* as you get? This is for real. I don't know what to make of it. Mama always says you're the brains of the family, so hey, get that big old Du Bois–educated noggin of yours down here, and I mean like yesterday."

I threw on some corduroys, a sweater, my black leather bomber jacket, hat, scarf, and gloves. Then I went out and cranked up my BMW, shivering more from the shock of waking up that early in the morning than anything else. The good thing about my beamer is that it's got a gorgeous hum when it's warming up. No shaking. No faking. Just a nice sweet, steady hum.

The bad thing is, it's too comfy. My body was engaged in a contest to see what would go to sleep first—my eyes or my legs. I had to turn the heat off and crack the window, that's just how unfocused I was.

That is till I walked into the Blues Box.

Sock it to me.

That's how I felt, because sitting there with a bottle of cognac and a shot glass was Angelina Rosseni.

She looked like Joe Frazier after tangling with Ali.

There was a black loop around her right eye, the cheekbone jutting out mountainous and gory. There was a slit in the bottom half of her lip, dividing two streams of bruises, one purple, the other crimson.

Her hands quivered and only steadied when she grabbed the bottle and the glass. Angelina gulped the liquor like a demon devouring a spirit.

Then she looked at me.

As a television journalist I've seen some sad eyes in my time y'all; eyes filled with grief after the death of a loved one or sorrow because of a burned-down house or gloom after a guilty verdict. I have looked into the eyes of the downhearted.

I can safely say that Angelina had the most stark combination of depression and fear I've glimpsed in years.

"Well," she wheezed, her voice spoiled by too much liquor, "I'm here."

"How'd you know to come here?" I asked.

"You said your sister owned this club, figured she'd know how to get to you, especially since you've been trying to get to me."

I pulled out the chair next to Angelina and sat down. Peaches stood behind her, at the bar, mesmerized.

Angelina said, "The world is looking for me, trying to hurt me, and I've landed on your doorstep."

"Who's looking to hurt you?"

Angelina glanced back at Peaches. "Can we talk alone?"

I looked at Peaches.

"*Oh but no.* Y'all are not gonna try and kick me out of my own place. *Wrong.*"

"C'mon, Peaches," I said, trying to look stern but pitiful.

"Oh, this is foul. You know that, right, sister-twin?"

I begged Peaches with my eyes.

"Are you gonna be okay?" Peaches asked, now more worried than insulted.

"I can handle it. I'll be okay. I'll call you as soon as I can."

Peaches glared at the back of Angelina's head. "And I gave you a free drink? You better act like you know up in here."

"Don't worry, Peaches, we'll be fine," I assured her.

"I'll lock the front. You go out the back way and make sure you lock up good too."

Then Peaches hugged me, and gave Angelina the *talk to the hand sign* behind her back. When she left, the room seemed to shrink to a cocoon with only Angelina and me in it.

"Okay, get to the point. Who wants to hurt you?"

"The police—they want to send me to jail."

"Why would they want to send you to jail?"

"Because I lied."

"About wh—"

"Horace—wants to kill me."

"Hightower? Why?"

"Because I know."

"You *lied* about what and you *know* about what, Angelina? Let me help you. You're already hurt, not just physically but emotionally. I see it in your eyes."

Angelina picked up the bottle. She was so nervous that she needed to use both hands. Angelina tried to pour and the neck shook, rattling against the rim of the shot glass. I reached out to steady the glass for her. Angelina grabbed it out of my hand and slung it against the wall.

The sweet, brown liquid lightly sprayed my face. The glass was wingless, falling to the ground in three cleanly cracked pieces.

"You're afraid. You're burdened. You're tired. Tired of lying and tired of holding in what you know. Get it off your chest, Angelina."

"I'm afraid," she mumbled. "He beat me up already."

"But if you tell the truth and help the police, you'll be all right. He won't be able to hurt you again."

Angelina reached down and pulled an envelope out of her bag. The mustard yellow folder had spots of dried blood on it. Angelina's blood. She wiped a tear from her eye, sniffed twice, and mumbled, "Can I have another glass?"

I touched her hand with mine and gave her a smile, before sliding my unused glass in front of her.

She successfully poured the drink this time. I opened the envelope as Angelina sipped.

"Looks like a draft," I said, confused. "For another will?"

"The new will, the one you talked about in your news story was about to be changed. Mr. Weaver was about to change it when he was murdered. Those are the notes he made."

I started to skim the draft as Angelina began to tell her story.

"I met Horace when I interviewed for the cleaning job. He sent me flowers and he took me to ritzy places. Bought me nice things. You know what I'm saying?"

"Sure, he wined and dined you. Every woman wants to be pampered. I feel you there, Angelina. But that was after you decided to go out with him. What drew you to Hightower in the first place?"

"Horace turned sixty-two this year, but he's got a body like a thirty-five-year-old. You've seen him. He came on to me strong. I liked his manliness. We became lovers but after several months Horace started to act kind of crazy. Moody. All into himself. The restaurants we went to weren't nice anymore. He got nervous and edgy."

Angelina began to cry. She dabbed at her eyes with the back of her hands.

"Take your time," I told her. "Take your time."

"Finally I got Horace to open up to me about three weeks ago. He said that Fab Weaver was acting distant, seemed to be trying to cut him off. Horace asked me to keep my eyes and ears open when I worked in the house. He'd been good to me so I did."

"And you found out something you had no business knowing, right?"

"Mr. Weaver had just asked me about cleaning up his son's apartment before some furniture was to be delivered. I said sure. I left something and doubled back. That's when I overheard him on the phone, talking. He was trying to find a new lawyer. He was writing out changes in his will, making detailed notes and stuff. If I knew what it would lead to, God, I never would have said a word."

Angelina stopped to devour the rest of the cognac in her glass.

"I told Horace what I knew and he just lost his mind. I've never seen him mad like that before. Horace said I had to help him. That he loved me. That if I helped him, he would be able to leave his wife and we could get married. All I had to do was get a couple of things for him. . . . Get those notes out of Mr. Weaver's study and, when I cleaned up Guy's apartment, steal his credit card."

"And you did it just like that?"

"I didn't know what he was going to do. It would be something shady, yeah, but I wasn't thinking murder!"

"Okay, okay. Go on, you found the credit card and . . ."

"The credit card was easy, finding the notes for the new will was hard. Mr. Weaver hid it pretty well. There's a secret compartment in his desk. I didn't find them until that morning you showed up."

"And Hightower was calling all the shots?"

"Yes. That's why I called Horace from the study: to tell him that I finally found the notes and that you were there."

"What did he say when you told him the media and the police were involved?"

"Horace told me to make sure that I acted normal. He told me what to say. He told me to be cooperative, don't do anything suspicious. Horace gave orders, he was in control at all times."

"Angelina, if Fab Weaver had gotten to a lawyer with these changes, Hightower wouldn't see a dime. It gives his fifty percent to a heart disease research center."

"That's why he wanted Mr. Weaver dead. He needed to keep the old will intact, so that he could get the money and stay in control."

"So how'd Hightower do it?"

"He used the credit card I stole to rent the car. Horace said all he was going to do was talk to Mr. Weaver that night, they were going to take a drive and he was going to try and reason with him. But I guess he couldn't."

"So reason turned into murder," I said. "How'd he get Jimmy Flamingo involved?"

"That I don't know. He just told me to make sure I told the cops about Jimmy threatening to kill Mr. Weaver, to describe Jimmy, and when the cops eventually brought him in, ID him. And I did."

"It's Jimmy's gun, his fingerprints are all over it. Why would he get mixed up with Hightower? And if Jimmy did cut a deal with Hightower to murder Fab Weaver, why'd Hightower double-cross him?"

"Horace probably offered him money, for going along, same as me. He can be so charming and persuasive! You don't know him. Horace can get you to do things you don't wanna do. And as far as the double cross goes, well, look at my face."

"Hightower's not only mean, Angelina, he's greedy. He set up Fab Weaver's son. With Guy in jail, he'd control all of the money."

"Once I was involved, I had to go along. Can't you see that? I had no idea that Horace could be so cold-blooded."

"After you ran away from me and Detective Eckart, why'd you go to him, knowing he was a killer? Huh, Angelina?"

"Where else could I go? I couldn't get the money out of the bank. The check wouldn't clear for another couple of days. I needed money. I thought he'd help me after I helped him. He said he loved me."

"And instead Hightower beat you."

Angelina began to sob gently, "He said that I blew it, that by running I tipped his hand. The only reason I'm still alive is because he knew I still had these notes. Horace wanted them. When we got in the car to go get them, I waited till we got to a stop sign at a crowded intersection, then I jumped out, screaming my head off, and ran through an alley. It was too risky for him to try and follow."

"So what brought you here to me, Angelina?"

"I was in a bar having a drink and I saw a rebroadcast of your ten o'clock news. That's when I decided to come to you."

"Now we need to go to the police."

Angelina began sobbing again. After she had a good cry, she stood up. I took her by the arm. We were heading out to the police station.

Angelina and I walked out to my car in the rear of the Blues Box. The only light was from the thick, metal streetlamp a foot away in the alley.

I looked up toward the security lamp that should have been on. The face was shattered and tiny pieces of jagged glass were all around the rim. I heard a crunching sound and looked down at our feet. Angelina was standing on broken glass, her back to me.

But Angelina wasn't moving her feet. The wild bush by the chain-link fence shook ever so slightly. I felt the flesh crawl on the back of my neck.

Somebody was out there. And I was doggone sure they didn't mean us no good.

"Run!" I shouted to Angelina as I headed back to the door of the Blues Box.

From behind, someone caught me with a forearm across the throat, a clothesline. With my momentum and their might, I flew backward hitting the ground with tremendous force. I saw speckled light as the pain shot from my ear to my head to my back, then to my legs. I saw Angelina open her mouth to scream. But the sound I heard was a gunshot as I fell back to the ground. I tried to turn to look, but couldn't, only glimpsing the heels of a man's shoes running away.

Then everything went black.

When I awoke, I was lying down in the back of an ambulance snorting smelling salts. I jerked up, blinking my eyes hard. Gentle but firm hands took ahold of my shoulders to push me back down, "Take it easy."

I craned my neck in time to see a black body bag being hoisted into a police paddy wagon. The little bit of run I had? That sight KO'd it. I fell back on the stretcher and sighed, "Oh God."

"Relax," the paramedic said. She was in her early fifties, I'd say. She had blond hair with streaks of sable, black eyes, and massive but soft hands. One of them was resting on my forehead. "Took a nasty knock on the head, no fever or anything. How do you feel?"

"Lucky that I'm not in a bag like Angelina."

"God is good, isn't He?" she said smiling.

"Yes, yes," I answered, feeling awfully grateful and blessed.

"Excuse me, ma'am?" a cop said to me, sticking his head into the ambulance. He was a detective, dressed in a heavy blue trench coat, badge hanging around his neck on a silver chain. "I need to ask you some questions."

I leaned up; my head throbbed just a little bit. "Okay, I'm ready."

Then he began to grill me about who Angelina was, why we were leaving the Blues Box after hours, what happened. I gave him as much info as I could. Then I told him that I was a reporter working the Fab Weaver murder case, that Angelina had been sought after by the police, that Doug was a personal friend of mine, and could he call him and have him meet us at the police station?

The brotherhood of the blue is the real deal. The detective took me to the station, handled me like something coveted and new.

"So you think," he said as we crossed the parking lot, heading into the cop shop, "that Horace Hightower murdered the victim . . . ah . . ."

"Angelina Rosseni," I said as he skimmed his notes.

"She was scared to death of him. You saw her bruises? Angelina said he did it. And now she's been shot to death and the draft for the new will is *missing!* It's a miracle he didn't shoot me too!"

"Well, don't worry, we'll get him."

They wouldn't have to.

We walked into the cop shop and there was Horace Hightower, standing there jawing it up with the desk sergeant, showing off a Rolex watch!

It took every fiber of my being not to jump on this man and knock *the living stew* out of him. I was seething. He was one bold *motor scooter!*

"Georgia," Doug said, standing in the doorway as cool as Shaft. I was not. My mad had surfaced to sea level. I was about to go off. "Georgia, be cool now."

"Be cool!" I echoed him.

"C'mon!" In a muscular yet balletic move, Doug swiftly reached my side. He grabbed me by the arm and pulled me into the interrogation room, preventing me from putting a Tae Bo hurtin' on Hightower.

"Me be cool?" the words bubbled inside my throat before roaring to the roof of my mouth. I told Doug what Angelina had told me about Hightower and the Fab Weaver murder. Then I added, "And now Angelina is dead. And I could be too. Then I walk in here and the man who did it is standing swapping *dick* stories with the desk sergeant."

"Georgia, baby, I'm always on your side. But let me tell you something. Horace Hightower is no lightweight. He's covered his tracks well. And he's got an airtight alibi for Angelina's murder."

"You're kiddin' me."

"He's been here since about two in the morning. Claims his car stopped on him about three blocks away from the station. Thought it was too dangerous to wait outside by a stranded Mercedes. Came in and sat on the bench right by the desk sergeant waiting for a tow. Best alibi in town."

I sat down, stunned. "But how? I was so sure . . ."

"Don't fret, girl. If you remember, we knew that there were two people in on this thing."

"Yeah, you guys are dead on Jimmy's case."

"But this is where Hightower the player overplayed his hand. Jimmy is in the hospital and no way could have come after Angelina. And, Hightower, he's been here. He can't be in two places at once."

"Right, right."

"So his *real* accomplice did the dirty work. Just like he did the dirty work earlier—killing Fab Weaver and helping set up Jimmy and Guy Weaver."

"Who?"

"Look what we just found out," Doug said, pulling out some notes that he had on this case. He showed me info on the gun that Jimmy had, which turned out to be the weapon used to murder Fab Weaver.

"Same gun, I know."

"Scored a match on the fingerprints with Jimmy. But—this right here is what you don't know. What does that say?"

"Another print was found."

"The shooter wiped off the gun, but forgot to get inside where you load the bullets. We found a thumbprint there and ran it through the computer."

"And you got a match!"

"Yes, ma'am. The guy had a record, an old conviction on a petty theft. Now, hold that thought." Then Doug flipped over a couple of pages and showed me a list.

"Look here, Georgia. These are the musicians who at one point or another threatened to file suit against Fab Weaver for stealing their songs."

I began reading out loud. "Paul 'Hound Dog' Watson. Jimmy 'Flamingo' Elm. Benjamin Albert Nelson Goodwin. Harriet 'Sugar' Wilson . . ."

"Back up one."

"Benjamin Albert Nelson Goodwin . . ."

"It's his print. That's our man."

"That's who, Doug?"

"Take the first initials from each name."

"B-A-N-G!" I stared at the paper in stunned silence. Finally I said, "I can't believe it."

"Believe it."

"Are you sure it's him? I thought Bang's last name was Robinson?"

"When Bang first came to Chicago he could only get work as a drummer. See, nobody liked his voice or that long name. Thought it was country. So he played around until he came up with Bang, thought it fit in real nice with the drumming too. He took the Robinson part from his favorite ballplayer, Jackie Robinson."

"How'd you find all that out?"

"The personal history? Just gleaned it out of him in the car, driving to the police station after leaving you and Peaches at the hospital. Some of it came out when we were just talking after he gave his police statement about Jimmy."

"And the lawsuit stuff? I didn't know Bang wrote music too, thought he just played drums."

"He wrote a couple of hits. And we had already begun looking at the people trying to sue Fab Weaver. I was able to track down some of the attorneys. Most didn't want to tangle with Fab Weaver and Horace Hightower."

"They were that powerful, huh?"

"Yep, and the case was tricky too; promised to be a long-drawn-out thing. Most of the attorneys said it wasn't likely that they would win. So they would look at the case, play with it, then eventually drop it."

"But?"

"But one attorney wanted to take a shot—Bang found him. He promised that he would really stick with the case. Dude's family is rich, so he didn't care that much about the money. But all of a sudden, Bang pulled out. Told the man to forget about it."

"That was shortly before Fab Weaver's murder?"

"Right. I figure he cut a deal with Horace Hightower. We're checking Bang's bank records now to see if he's made any big deposits."

"Bang and Hightower. Well, how come Hightower is out there chilling showing off his Rolex watch instead of shaking in his BVDs sporting handcuffs?"

"'Cause we don't have anything on him that's hard evidence, that's why. Your secondhand story from Angelina is helpful but won't stand up in court by itself. Told you about Hightower's alibi for her murder. When I nail Hightower I want it to be damn good."

"Well, how are we going to do that, Doug?"

"I've got a plan. We've got Bang and he'll give up Hightower for sure. The allegiance will no longer make sense. But I need your help. Are you up to it, lady?"

"I'm in."

"Good," Doug smiled. "Because I need you to pull one more person in with us."

Chapter Twenty-one

A PRISM OF LIGHT PIERCED THE WINDOWPANES, GIVING color to the swarthy casket. Inside this room there was drunken silence, weighty and unfeeling.

Twelve people came to say goodbye that evening and seemed absolutely content to merely say it with their presence. No sobs were heard. No tears were seen falling.

There was a larger crowd in the vestibule—a crowd with names that appeared as bylines in daily newspapers or nightly on the evening news.

The average person just might balk at the sight of the media lingering outside a funeral service.

But we came to cover a story. If the story somehow involved something that many people held sacred, well, there was nothing we could do about it. We came to tell the story of the thorn, not the rose.

The media was looking to talk to Horace Hightower.

He was one of the twelve who came to say goodbye to Fab Weaver.

Guy Weaver was also one of the twelve.

I was standing near a rear door, peeping in as the service neared completion. The funeral parlor's staff quietly closed the casket. They rolled the body out to the car. There were no pallbearers.

Apparently the weight of Fab Weaver's earthly deeds was too much to carry.

I watched as Guy spoke to Horace Hightower. He seemed assured and extremely confident. Hightower listened intently, nodding, hooked on his client's every word. To those who did not know, it would seem that the two were sharing a cherished moment about the person they both had come to mourn.

Hightower got up and began walking behind the casket. Guy followed, his head hanging wearily. Briefly, like the flutter of wings, our eyes met.

Guy had planted the seed.

Now it was up to me to tend the garden.

Outside, television microphones sprang up aggressively as the crowd surrounded Horace Hightower. Dude was cool. A Frigidaire in a man's suit. *Cool, baby, cool.* I let my colleagues soften him up with some body punches.

"Mr. Hightower, what do you think about the murder of Angelina Rosseni?"

"I think it's a shame. Any loss of life such as this seems so senseless. Ms. Rosseni was a valued worker. She was outstanding at what she did. Her murder was tragic."

"Was it a personal tragedy for you?"

"Personal in the sense that someone I came in contact with has been murdered, yes."

"What was the nature of your personal relationship with the victim?"

Another reporter shouted, "He means did you have an affair with her?"

"No comment."

"Does that mean yes?"

"It means no comment."

"Do you think her murder is related to the killing of Fab Weaver?"

"That's something you should ask the police, not me."

Like Maceo's horn was a cue for James Brown to do his thang, that question gave me the opening I needed to start firing off my questions.

"Guy Weaver's been charged with his father's murder. Police will probably charge Jimmy Flamingo too should he recover. There seems to be no link between these two men; could they be innocent? Could there be another suspect out there that the police should be going after?"

"I have no way of knowing that. That's something the police have to find out, but they have not indicated to me that they were looking for any more suspects."

"But don't you think that because of Fab Weaver's money, power, and cutthroat nature that there could have been more than one person who wanted him dead?"

"All I know are the facts. One: Police have the gun that killed my client. Two: That weapon belongs to Jimmy Flamingo and has his fingerprints all over it. And three: He also threatened to kill Mr. Weaver and myself on a number of occasions."

Our eye contact was steady and long. Then Hightower broke our gaze and began to head for his car. "No more questions, please. Thank you."

We all watched Hightower get in his silver-colored Mercedes and speed away.

One of the reporters from the *Chicago Tribune* asked me, "Where were you trying to go with that?"

"Nowhere really"—I shrugged—"just fishing." Then I dropped my eyes and smiled to myself.

Guy told Hightower that Doug had called him and said that he would be cleared soon, that they had a line on a new suspect and were closing in. When Hightower asked who? Guy told him that Doug wouldn't say any more than that.

Now all that was true blue *except* for one itsy-bitsy thing. I was the one who convinced Guy to tell the story to Hightower. He was the one that Doug wanted me to help reel in so we could crack this murder case. Guy's sizzling tidbit plus the *whamma-jamma* I put on Hightower's mind during the media gangbang had the boy going for sure.

Good doggone thing too.

The cops had put a tail on Hightower. Mr. Thang went back to his office. Then about an hour later he came tearing out of there. The undercover crew gleaned that Hightower was heading *my way*.

My way was a vacant building across the street from Bang's Game Room on Record Row. I was there with Zeke, stationed by a side window. It was us, and, of course, a police surveillance crew.

The police surveillance crew had spent most of the day setting up this sting operation. Zeke and I had a great shot of the equipment rigged up to show the inside of the Game Room. Bang was sitting behind the bar waiting.

One of the police officers spoke to Doug over the two-way radio: "Hightower should be here within minutes. Picture's dead on."

"Gotcha," I heard Doug answer back over the two-way. He was inside staked out in the rear storeroom along with two other detectives. There was also an undercover car parked across the street; another one was parked in the alley behind the building.

"Hey," the leader of the surveillance crew asked over the two-way, "are you sure we won't have anyone dropping in? I don't want us to get caught with a thumb up our ass!"

"No way," Doug answered. "Bang called all his regulars and told them that the Game Room would be closed today, and we took the phone off the hook."

"Good deal, Doug. It's a waiting game now." Then the cop laughed before continuing. "Say, our friend Bang, he don't look so hot!"

That's because Doug had hauled Bang in by the scruff of his

raggedy neck; boyfriend had the nerve to try to shoot at the police too! All Bang got for his trouble was a beat-down once the detectives got ahold of him.

Bang was the missing link and was about as smart as one. After being grilled about his part in the murder, and being shown the evidence against him—which, by the way, was stacking up as neat as a row of dime pancakes—Bang decided to act like he was born with a little bit of sense.

Hightower drove the car and helped to dump the body in the lake. But it turns out that Bang is the Kunta Kinte of crime—he did all the heavy lifting and all the dirty work. No kidding, baby. Bang got a phony license, rented the car, did the shooting, and tossed the body in the lake with Hightower. Bang would also be the one to take a jail-house bow for it all too—unless, Doug assured him, he wore a wire to catch Hightower.

Bang didn't require too much convincing once he realized that Death Row ain't no song and dance, excuse my pun. He agreed to wear a wire. All Doug and I had to do was bait Hightower well enough to get him to come and confront Bang.

For my help convincing Guy to cooperate with the police and properly rattle Hightower's cage, I was rewarded by being allowed to exclusively film the bust. I was cutting up something fierce getting this killer exclusive. I was sitting as pretty as a diva on the cover of *Essence*.

"Hey, Georgia," Zeke asked, "what did Bang say to Hightower over the phone?"

"Well, according to Doug, Hightower told Bang that the police must be on to him. He told Bang that he needed to get out of town."

"Boy, he swallowed the bait and the reel," Zeke laughed.

The cop heading up the surveillance team jumped in. "Yep. But you know it's funny. I've found that these criminals are always nervous, always looking over their shoulders. They know they've done wrong. They don't wanna get caught but they're always expecting something to go wrong—something that'll get them caught."

"And that," I reasoned out loud, "causes them to make mistakes."

Zeke gave me a thumbs-up in agreement.

"Heads up, Robocops!" one of the officers said. "Hightower's rolling up now. Jesus! Look at that sweet Mercy-d! Hope to God that ends up for sale at the police auction."

We watched as the silver limited-edition vehicle turned into the side alley and parked. Hightower got out and didn't even look up; a scowl marred the lower quarter of his face. Hightower had a baseball cap pulled down over his eyes and was wearing a cloth baseball jacket, also black, and dark jeans. His hands were jammed into his pockets.

The surveillance camera picked him up on the inside. The equipment was recording and Zeke was shooting the monitor as we all watched. The picture was a bit grainy but the audio was flawless.

"What the hell is going on, Bang?" Hightower growled, whipping his cap off to smack the counter with it. Then he began wiping his sweaty brow with the crook of his arm. "You screwed up."

"Screwed up what?" Bang said, so innocently it sounded stiff and funny.

One of the cops working surveillance with us grunted, "What a pitiful acting job."

"He ain't no Denzel Washington," Zeke said sarcastically.

"Not even a Spike Lee! Let's hope his acting gets better so he can pull this off," I said, rooting for Bang. "C'mon, Bang. Work, boy, work."

"Hightower, man, what's the deal?"

He pointed his finger in Bang's direction, "You. You're the deal— a done deal. Guy said the police are going to drop the charges against him. He said they have some kind of a lead they're sure will clear him. And that bitchy reporter broad . . ."

"Don't hate," I said. I smiled, liking that I had gotten under my man's skin.

". . . she hinted around that there were maybe more suspects. You've got to get out of town and fast."

"Why are you so worried?" Bang asked. "You helped dump the body but I did the actual shooting, remember?"

Hightower glared at him.

"I mean why are you so scared? I've got everything on the line. You just planned everything—to get the fake license, the credit card, and all that, but I had to do all the dirty work, right?"

Hightower leaned across the counter and grabbed Bang by the shirt and yanked him forward. "Don't give me a goddamn hard time, okay?"

"Shit!" one of the cops watching the surveillance monitor barked. "Watch the hookup under the shirt!"

"What's the matter with you, Bang? You're acting funny and I don't like it one bit."

The picture began to scramble. Speckled egg-colored snow filled the monitor and then the audio began to hiss.

"C'mon, you jerk. Let him go before you yank the entire connection loose!"

Now all of us were leaning in watching the monitor flare up and settle down, flare up and settle down.

"Bang, if you think I'm going to jail because you're stupid you've got another think coming. Now I'll give you all the money you need, just—"

Hightower's voice dropped low. The picture on the surveillance monitor cleared up. "What the hell is that stuck to your chest?"

"Busted!" Zeke cussed under his breath.

Hightower started to run for the front door. "You sonofabitch!"

Doug and two of his men came out of the storeroom, guns drawn. "Police! Hold it, Hightower."

"Baker Ten on the street to Surveillance Team One—there's somebody heading into the joint!"

Our heads jerked up and we looked out the window. Who do we see tearing their way toward the Game Room?

"Peaches! No!" I shouted like she could hear me through brick and glass. *What is she doing?*

I leaned my reporter mug all the way into the monitor as Peaches went gangbusters through that doorway.

Hightower grabbed her by the arm, jerked her in front of him, and pulled a gun out of his pocket. "Now you hold it!"

Peaches was panting, "Aww, this ain't my kind of a party, y'all! What's going on? Bang!"

"Shut up!" Hightower shouted, his gun hand shaking.

My heart lurched forward. I thought, Awww, Peaches girl, you got worse timing than a busted wristwatch!

Zeke put his arm around my shoulders. "Stay calm. Doug's in there."

"Let her go!" Doug ordered, taking a step forward. "You'll never make it. Go easy now and we'll go easy later, how about it?"

"How about I take this hostage and get the hell out of here."

"That's bullshit, Hightower. I'm not playing with you," Doug growled. "If you hurt her, I won't rest until your ass is mine, understand?"

"Give up, man, we're busted!" Bang pleaded. "Ain't no need of making it any worse than it is."

Hightower was panting nervously, but as soon as he heard Bang's words, he swallowed hard, swiveled left behind Peaches, then fired! The bullet caught Bang in the shoulder. He yelled and clutched his arm just as he began falling forward onto the bar.

Peaches screamed her head off!

"Hold-hold-hold!" Doug yelled to his men. "Hold your fire!"

Hightower clutched Peaches and began backing out of the Game Room.

"He's getting away!" I heard myself moan, and then I just ran. . . . I heard Zeke calling my name and other voices yelling for me to stop. But how could I? That's my twin! I ran out the door and down one flight of stairs, stopping only when I reached the doorway to the street.

"Are you nuts!" a cop shouted as soon as he laid eyes on me. He grabbed me and pulled me down behind an undercover car. His gun was drawn, his eyes steady on the target.

That target was Hightower, who was now fully backed out of the building, dragging Peaches by the neck and the scruff of her heels.

"Hold it!" one of the street cops shouted.

Hightower jerked himself and Peaches around. He looked stunned as he realized that there were four sets of pistols aimed at him outside while Doug and his boys were still advancing front side. Fear stiffened Hightower's body and I noticed that he loosened his grip around Peaches' neck. "Run, twin!" I yelled at the top of my lungs.

Peaches bit down on Hightower's arm and broke away.

He screamed, swinging his gun hand high in the air in the direction of the cops standing near the alley. The gun went off.

One of the cops returned fire and the bullet grazed Hightower's forehead. He fell to the ground and rolled behind the trunk of a car, parked at the curb.

Peaches was now safely out of the line of fire. One of the officers had grabbed her and tucked her behind the building.

"Let Hightower see some smoke, fellahs!" Doug yelled. The cops opened fire, tearing into that car. A rapid-fire pinging sound filled the air. Dime-sized holes began to appear in the metal. They were missing on purpose, but Hightower covered his head with both his hands. He tossed the gun forward. It landed on the ground, clanking and bouncing like a broken marble.

Doug shouted, "Hold your fire! Hold your fire!"

"Don't shoot! I'm unarmed!" Hightower said, struggling to his feet, holding his arms up, stumbling forward. There was a tiny stream of blood trickling down his forehead.

Doug ran toward him.

Hightower dabbed at a tiny cut on his forehead. "Help me," he groaned. "I'm hurt!"

"Not enough for me!" Doug said, hitting him in the jaw with a right cross. Doug stared at Hightower after he hit the ground. "Somebody read this jerk his rights when he comes to, huh?"

———

GOD DON'T LIKE UGLY.

And what Bang and Hightower did sure wasn't pretty.

Adultery. Stealing. Lying. Cheating. Killing.

If the commandments were a mirror, the two of them cracked it with a brick.

But they're due for a lot more than seven years of bad luck.

More like twenty-five years to life.

You see our plan played out perfectly in a doubly blessed manner.

First: we caught the bad guys and put them away.

Two: Jimmy came out of his coma!

That's why Peaches had gone to the Game Room. She wanted to share the good news with Bang, but she couldn't get an answer because the phone was off the hook. That's how Peaches got caught in a rundown.

But I swear when my twin burst into that shop and Hightower put that gun to her big old waterhead—wheez, you could have knocked me out with a feather.

Thank God Doug and his *police posse* know how to handle their business.

Afterward Peaches had the nerve to ask me, "Did I look scared, sister-twin?"

I asked her, "Is a bull beef?" *Please!*

Story Slug = Weaver Folo
5 P.M. Show, December 15th

ANCHOR INTRO

(DAN READS)

CLOSE-UP

A new development tonight in the Fab Weaver murder case.

You'll recall Bang Robinson and Horace Hightower were arrested just a few days ago. They were charged with Fab Weaver's murder and that of Angelina Rosseni.

WJIV's Georgia Barnett is live at the criminal courts building with late details. Georgia?

(*********STOP*********)

TAKE LIVE SHOT

CHYRON LOCATION:

LIVE/CRIMINAL COURTS BLDG.

LIVE/GEORGIA BARNETT/CHANNEL 8 NEWS

(GEORGIA LIVE)

Thanks, Dan.

It was a complicated conspiracy—involving old grudges, millions of dollars in record royalties, an extramarital affair, and, of course, a double murder.

Just a short time ago, prosecutors cut a deal with one of the suspects.

(*******STOP*********)**

TAKE PACKAGE
GEORGIA ON TAPE

FIRST B-ROLL SHOT OF BANG IN CUFFS
BEING LED BY POLICE.

"That suspect is this man, Bang Robinson, shown here being led from the Criminal Courts Building by police."

CUT TO B-ROLL SHOT OF UNDERCOVER
SURVEILLANCE VIDEO OF BANG TALKING
WITH HIGHTOWER.

"He was arrested for being the gunman who shot and killed Fab Weaver. As evidence began to pile up, Bang Robinson agreed to wear a wire to catch the person police say is the mastermind behind the plot. Police say Bang Robinson was the trigger man, angry with Weaver about stolen royalties for songs he'd written in the sixties on Chicago's famed Record Row."

TAKE SHOT OF PHOTO OF ANGELINA.

"Robinson has also admitted to shooting and killing Angelina Rosseni, claiming Horace Hightower ordered the murder. Hightower and Rosseni were having an extramarital affair and she allegedly helped him pull off the Fab Weaver murder plot."

TAKE MORE B-ROLL SHOT OF BANG WALKING.

"Because Bang Robinson has given a detailed confession, worn a wire, and will testify against Horace Hightower, prosecutors will not seek the death penalty in his case."

**TAKE B-ROLL SHOT OF HIGHTOWER'S
OFFICE/NAME ON DOOR.**

"Prosecutors say because of Robinson's detailed confession and the incriminating surveillance video, no bail was set for the other suspect in this case, attorney Horace Hightower."

**TAKE B-ROLL SHOT OF HIGHTOWER
BEING ARRESTED.**

"Hightower, shown here struggling with police, is behind bars tonight. He claims that he is innocent and did not know that Bang Robinson was going to murder Fab Weaver. He has hired three well-known Chicago lawyers—a Midwest dream team if you will."

**TAKE B-ROLL SHOT OF HOME VIDEO OF
JIMMY'S DEBUT AT THE BLUES BOX.**

"Cleared of any wrong doing in this case are two men who earlier were named as suspects. They are Blues guitarist Jimmy Flamingo, who is recovering from a drug overdose . . .

**PHOTO OF GUY WEAVER, COURTESY
CHICAGO SUN-TIMES.**

. . . and Guy Weaver, the victim's son, who was once considered a prime suspect.

PLAYBILL OF JIMMY FLAMINGO.

Jimmy Flamingo vows to return to the stage next month with a performance at the Blues Box."

**TAKE B-ROLL SHOT OF GUY
WALKING TO A
LIMO AT HIS FATHER'S FUNERAL.**

"And Guy Weaver, Fab Weaver's son, is now making efforts to pay back money to the musicians that his father cheated. Weaver, recovering from drug addiction, says that he wants his life clean in all ways."

DUMP TAPE TAKE GEORGIA LIVE

(GEORGIA LIVE)

"This murder case has generated new interest in Chicago's Record Row and the sad plight of some of the musicians who made it famous. There is talk of building a three-story music center on South Michigan Avenue, one that would house gold records, photos, and even offer music classes for children. Part of the money generated by the center would go toward health benefits for aging musicians.

"Live from the Criminal Courts Building, I'm Georgia Barnett. Channel 8 News."